SKY MOON

SKY MOON
C. C. VAUGHAN

Castlebrook Publications
Santa Rosa, California

Castlebrook Publications

Castlebrook Publications
1535 Farmers Lane, PMB 237
Santa Rosa, CA 95405
www.castlebrookbooks.com
www.youdrawitbooks.com
e-mail castlebrookbooks@aol.com

Sky Moon is a work of fiction. Names, characters, places, and
incidents are the products of the author's imagination or are
used fictitiously. Any resemblance to actual events, locales, or
persons, living or dead, is entirely coincidental.

Cover photo courtesy of www.freenaturepictures.com/moon-
pictures.php
Cover design and book design Christina Vaughan

To my dear and loving husband, Robert Ellis,
who encourages me in my writing and who reads
every one of my books, even my children's books
and
To my wonderful and loving son, Colin Lipper,
who has been a blessing in my life from day one
and
In memory of my father, George Clay Vaughan,
who implanted the idea in me of being a writer
by telling me he gave his first three children middle names
which he thought would make our names good pen names,
such as Christina Clayton Vaughan,
in case any of us should become a writer
and
In memory of my mother, Melanie Constance Papajohn Vaughan,
who was an avid reader and always had plenty of
classic literature in the house for me to explore.
She had one book, however, not considered among
the classics, which counterbalanced the classic influence
on me and led me down a lifelong path of
questioning classic reality.
That book was Eric von Daniken's
Chariots of the Gods

John Davis stared out his office window. A gray blanket of clouds shrouded the San Francisco skyline. It was a lackluster day inside and out. Nothing unusual in the way of news coming into the *Bay View* newsroom. The same old murders, accidents, drive-by shootings, political wranglings. John's attention turned inward, his thoughts echoing the depressing gray outside.

What has happened to my big dreams, the novels, the Nobel Prize for Literature, the screenplays that would win Academy Awards? I can't seem to even find the dreams any more, much less write anything that isn't totally trite. What happened to my "Golden Boy" status, conferred on me by my classmates in the yearbook? Seems all I have of it is the golden hair, and even that is fading to gray.

"… John! Hey, John, wake up! Back to reality now…" It was his friend and fellow news slave Brad, aka Bradford Harrison Scott, a short, wiry fellow with dark curly hair.

A pretentious name, John mused to himself, turning around in his chair. He pretended to be alert and upbeat. "What's up?"

Brad waved an envelope in John's direction. "A hot and heavy news story, no doubt, ha, ha—addressed to some guy named John. No last name. Could that be you? Some hottie writing you love letters?"

John feigned disinterest, but his mind snapped back from his depressing thoughts to alertness. Anything even slightly out of the ordinary around this noisy but boring place could, and in this case did, intrigue him. "Must be some other John. We got another John somewhere?"

"Nope. You, and only you, lover boy." Brad dropped the envelope on the desk, plopped down in the chair across from John, and waited expectantly for him to open the plain white envelope.

Unmoving, John stared down at the envelope addressed in a cultivated, feminine handwriting. "This your idea of a joke, Bradley?"

"Bradford to you—no! Mister Scott to you, ha ha. It's no joke, on my part, anyway. Came in today's mail. Aren't you going to open it?"

"I think you have too much enthusiasm for this place. If you're not careful, we'll all have to start working harder."

Brad laughed. "Come on, John, don't keep me in suspense. Open it."

John picked up the envelope and slit it with his letter opener. "You don't need to wait around, Bradley. If this turns out to be the story of the year, I'm certainly not going to share it with you."

Brad smiled and remained in his chair. John pulled a folded sheet of white paper out of the envelope. It had handwriting on both sides. A photograph slipped out onto the desk. Brad snatched it up, perused it with a raised eyebrow. "Hmm… not bad, not bad at all. Where'd you meet her?" He handed the photo to John, who stared at it as if hypnotized.

John shook his head slightly, then laid the photo on the desk. "I don't know. She looks familiar, but I don't remember meeting her."

"I don't know how you could forget a woman like that." Brad watched him as he read the letter. First John's eyes widened a bit, then a smile broke across his face, then he chuckled.

"What is it, man? Read it to me. I wanna laugh, too."

John continued reading in silence. At one point he picked up the photo again and perused it carefully, then went back to the letter.

November 9th

Dear John:
I saw you on television. I recognized you immediately.
Unfortunately, I can't remember your last name. Somewhere
in the distant past we met somewhere in a dimly lit room.
However, I don't think it was in this lifetime. Do you
remember writing some articles called the "Chronicles"? Back

in the forties? Even though it was another lifetime, I feel I know you, that you are the only person in the world I can talk to. I can't talk to my psychiatrist, or anyone else in this insane asylum. They already think I'm insane. If I say anything at all, I'll just dig myself in deeper here, and never, ever will they let me out. It was talking to my psychiatrist that got me in here in the first place.

I'm not sure why. It's so confusing. I think they are trying to confuse me on purpose. I have a feeling I am being kept here because I know something very important. They want me to think I'm crazy. Am I crazy? I'm afraid I can't answer yes or no, but either I am crazy, or I am not. There is no in between. If I am crazy, thank God, because then the world will not be destroyed. The horrible impending doom will not come about. If I am not crazy, then someone who can do something about the future must know what will happen. I certainly can't do anything about it in here. I can't believe my psychiatrist put me in here. I feel so betrayed. They want you to tell them your deepest, darkest secrets and then they lock you up.

I am sending you a picture of me. If you feel any sense of recognition, I hope you will try to keep an open mind about the things I have to tell you. Even if you are sure you have never seen me before, I hope you will read what I have to say. If you don't believe me, maybe you will at least be entertained by my letters. But you've got to believe me and do something about it! The future of the world rests on our shoulders!

It's going to take a lot of writing to tell you everything. If you're not willing to read it, I am not willing to write it, because for sure no one else will want to read it, and why waste my time writing to a brick wall. So, please write back and let me know if it is okay to write you again.

Sincerely yours,
Christina

"Come on, Davis. Tell me. What's it say?"
"Nothing. It's just some nut case in a mental hospital with

delusions. Your everyday doomsday warning." Even so, he carefully returned the letter and the picture to the envelope, stood up and put on his jacket, stuffed the letter in the inside breast pocket. Hair a little gray or not, tall and lean, John still had a certain boyish charm, a glint of humor in his blue eyes.

"Let's get some lunch."

When John arrived home that evening, he did nothing about the letter but toss it on a heap of papers on his desk, which he had given up using to write the screenplay of the century, which he couldn't get to work out logically after the first page. It seemed to him that the "logic" gene was too dominant to allow him the flights of fancy necessary for that kind of success.

—⁓—

Another week had gone by, each day pretty much the same as the week before, except that the ever-present blanket of clouds dropped three inches of rain on the City. John picked up the pile of mail from the mail slot labeled "News Desk" and rifled through it. Halfway through, he caught himself looking for another envelope addressed to "John." In every case, though, the envelopes were simply addressed to "News Desk." He put them back in the mail slot. He knew from experience that these letters would be a waste of time. Anything important, real, or serious was phoned in, faxed, or e-mailed.

Lost in thought and tuned out from the chatter of the newsroom staff, he ambled to the break room, poured himself a cup of coffee, and headed for his desk. There, in an almost hypnotic state, he felt called by his computer to focus on it. He checked his e-mail. No e-mails except in his spam folder. He scanned the spam subjects. "Hiiii, John!!!" caught his eye. Probably something that was just waiting for him to open it to give his computer and all the newspaper's computers a virus. *Never open spam.* He opened it. His desire was so hidden to hear from Christina, he was barely aware of what he had hoped to find, but find it he did.

November 16th

Dear John:
I haven't heard from you yet. Perhaps you need more time to think about responding, so I will go on with one more letter, and maybe it will help you make up your mind. My friend's brother brought his laptop and said I could use it while he was visiting his sister here. Now if they just don't come in my room and catch me, I can really get into telling you what has happened to me. I hope I have your correct e-mail address. This was the only one belonging to a reporter in the newsroom with the first name John. Davis. John Davis. I guess you're not Jewish?

"Why is she asking that?" John accidentally said aloud. He glanced cautiously around the room. No one was paying any attention to him. He went on reading, his heart pounding for a reason he wasn't quite aware of, or didn't want to admit to.

Where to start to tell you? Where did I start? It's getting hard to determine my own original birth date and place of origin. I thought it was 1947, but now I'm not so sure. There's the problem of continuation, the continuum. Where were you in 1000 CE? (Used to be A.D.— see how time changes, even the past?) It matters little at the moment, whenever this moment is. Even the time question is up for grabs, relatively speaking. Yes, 1947 was the year of the mysterious crash in June near Roswell, New Mexico. I think it was more than just a coincidence I was born not long before that. I think they were coming to look for me even then, but what happened? Who stopped them? Somebody made a big mistake, and they are still trying to rectify it. There was another, less publicized, UFO sighting the very night I was born. I don't know what it has to do with me, but, something, yes... something.
Maybe I should start more recently in Larkspur, California. It was in November. November seems to be the month I fall in love most often. Perhaps the month had

something to do with it, although it was not really love this time that I fell into. It was something much worse. Until then, I thought I was normal. Well, no, I didn't always think I was normal. I had just conveniently forgotten I was not normal, ever.

Anyway, the day was over, it was about eleven when I turned out the light and closed my eyes. You may think what happened next was just a dream. Or you may think it was a memory—a genetic memory, or a past life memory, or an astral–travel–to–the–past memory, or anything but real here–and–now reality. But time is an illusion, and, as such, is my only hope of salvation and the only hope of salvation of the world. When they say everything is now and that there is really no time or space, you'd better believe it is so.

The next thing I knew—after I closed my eyes to go to sleep, in case you've forgotten—I was walking into what looked like an old library. The lighting was rather dim, more like a nightclub. I don't know where I was. I looked down at my old-fashioned clothes and wondered what I was doing in them—and with such large breasts! They weren't abnormally large, certainly not, but much larger than I am used to having! I was wearing a forties' style dress, and a very large-brimmed hat. I was around thirty years old. I knew the people there, except for one man— you! It was the usual, corny pulp fiction thing— our eyes met across the room and an electrical charge passed between us. You know, the love at first sight thing. Like we had known each other forever. My friend came up to me and said you wanted to meet me, so she introduced us.

Before your name came out of her mouth, I knew it. John. You were very handsome, tall, golden-toned skin, golden hair.

You came up close to me, your eyes on mine all the way. You seemed to glow all over, especially your eyes. They were as blue as a Mediterranean sky. Your lips moved toward mine, under my big hat. No one would have seen us kiss, with my big hat in the way, but I resisted. Thought I had some crumbs on the edges of

my mouth, maybe bad breath, and what the hell was
going on anyway? I couldn't kiss a man I had just at that
moment met. I said, "I think this is rushing it a bit, do you
think we could get to know each other first?" You smiled
a little and walked over to the table and said, "I want to
show you something I've written. It was published in the
Bay View." I looked at it, but I couldn't make much out
about it. As I said before, the light was dim. The article
was called "Chronicles." It had something to do with a
Jewish center in Marin County. It was a big deal, seemed
to encompass all the great things Jews have done
throughout the centuries. Were you Jewish back then? It
seems I fall for Jewish men more often than not, no matter how I tried to get away from them. Really, all I wanted
was someone with a similar background to mine. No
more decorating the Christmas tree by myself and feeling guilty because I had a different self. Well, I thought,
at least he's a writer like me. We'd have something in
common. (Actually I have tried writing, but with no publishing success, and no success at writing anything even
half good.)

I had to go to the bathroom, so I excused myself to go
find one. I didn't have a clue where I was, so it wasn't
easy to find, but I found one. On my way back, I passed
a kiosk of sundries for sale. (Do you know what sundries
are? Well, look it up. I'm not going to tell you.) I looked
in my purse. I had only one cigarette left in a pack. (No,
I don't smoke now in this lifetime.) I bought a new pack.
Then I returned to where you were, only you were gone.
The man who could sweep me off my feet was gone! He
couldn't wait five minutes! My friend told me you had to
leave, but that I would definitely see you again. When,
ha! is what I'd like to know. Looks like sixty something
years later, I'm still waiting to see you again. Although, as
it turns out, it's for a reason more important than sexual
attraction. (Although I have a feeling that the attraction
will still be there.)

Anyway, I left for home with my friends. The next thing
I knew, it was the nineties. We were in my white Jeep

Cherokee Wagon. (I don't really have one.) Dreams and Reality are very confused. I was a young woman, much younger than I ought to be if I was born in 1947. I pulled up to my "dream" house overlooking the San Francisco Bay. As we got out of the Cherokee, we saw a tremendous spaceship in the sky over the Bay. All we could do was scream, "OH, MY GOD!" We knew our world had at this moment, changed irrevocably forever and there wasn't a thing we could do about it.

The spaceship was in two parts, the underneath half narrower but still as long as the top part. The two parts did not seem to be connected to each other by visible means, but they were somehow one ship.

I went in the door to the laundry room. I put my purse on the dryer and took off my flowered jacket and put it on top of my purse. I went out to the car again. The others were still looking at the space ship. Then this alien— or was he human—in a white helmet and a gas mask contraption and a strange gun—maybe a laser gun—and a couple of others were with him, but he seemed to be in charge—he said we were to come with him.

They were going to transform us—how or to what I did not then know. I just knew it wasn't good and I didn't want it. He grabbed me by the arm. I was acting on instinct, so the outcome of the next step I took did not really occur in my mind. It was just action, one after another. I asked if I could get my jacket as it was chilly out. He said okay and released his grip on my arm. Well, I stepped through the door into the laundry room, got the jacket and put it on. I looked in my purse. There was one new pack of cigarettes and a pack with only one left, and a lighter. I don't know how they got there, didn't know I smoked. Didn't know if I didn't. I think they were somehow left over from the forties.

Something had happened to my mind when I saw that spaceship, like some different neural pathways suddenly became activated. I took the cigarettes and lighter out of my purse and stuck one pack in each of the two side pockets of my jacket. For some reason I thought

they would come in handy. I also took the cash out of
my purse. I stashed my purse behind the washer. If they
couldn't find my ID, maybe they couldn't identify me. I felt
they were looking for me specifically.

Then I ran through the house, out the patio door, and
escaped. I ran down the hill toward the City. The first
thing I came to was a small park with a few trees and
some grass. Two guys were lounging in the grass. It was
right near the bay. As I approached the park, I noticed I
was in my bare feet. I suddenly rose up off the ground.
I realized I could fly, or at least levitate. I thought I must
have already been transformed. Had I received this power by being touched by the alien? Somehow I didn't think
he had in mind a positive type of transformation, but here
I was already transforming in a very positive way. I felt
they would find me, knew they could, because they could
home in on me, knowing the exact, individual magnetic
resonance of my DNA or something. Where I got this
idea, I don't know. But I knew they could track me.

There seemed to be a lot of information in my mind
I hadn't been aware of before. I tried to call out to the
guys below—it was a combined desire for help—and I
found myself realizing that indeed the whole world could
change for the better that day if everyone knew they
could fly. So I stretched out my arms to tell the news to
the world, starting with these two men. "Look! I can fly!"
I called out to them. They looked right at me, but their
expressions didn't change, like they were watching a
movie or something. I couldn't talk very loud—it was a
real effort because I was enmeshed in TERROR of the
aliens who were no doubt searching for me. I was so
tired and frustrated and scared. I knew that no matter
where I went, even if I could fly, they would eventually
come and get me.

And soon the alien did come and with a strange power
sucked me out of the air somehow and he took me with
him. Was he really an alien, or was he a government
agent? Because I had seen the space ship, I assumed
he was an alien. It was only later that I began to wonder.

The next thing I remember, we were in front of these glass doors where the transformation room was. The doors fronted the city street, with other buildings all around. It seemed to me that everything, including the street, was indoors or even underground.

He pushed me inside. A human-looking man was waiting for me. He was the only person I saw there except for the transformees. He looked Chinese. He said, "Let's get on with your transformation. The others have already begun." He showed me the rack where people were hung on hangers after they were transformed. They had body hair like monkeys. Naked, no legs below mid-thigh, arms only to the elbows. No feet. No hands. Long faces, and the front one had long dark brown hair and a silly grin on her face. Oh, God, I thought, she looked like me. They were all females that I could see, with large, pointy breasts sticking out from the fur. Is this what they want to do to me? Turn me into some sort of toy? What perverted race of aliens were they selling "transformed" humans to?

I could not possibly go through this transformation. The man came toward me with a syringe. My instincts took over.

"Wait a minute! I haven't had a cigarette in a long time and I know I won't have any ever again, so could I have one last cigarette?" I don't think I'd smoked since the forties, but he didn't know that. There was a single cigarette loose in my pocket. I grabbed it and held the lighter to it before he could answer. He hesitated. I had surprised him. He seemed to soften a little. Was that a hint of compassion? He said, "I don't want the others to know." Would they tell on him that he wasn't ruthless enough? He must be human. Maybe the aliens were forcing him to work for them, carrying out their nefarious plans. I looked around for "the others." A woman and a young boy. They also looked Chinese. Were they his family? Were the aliens using them as hostages to keep him working for them?

I snatched at the small opening in his heart. "Course not. I'll just step outside the door and smoke it." I stepped out quickly, before he could answer. Why he didn't follow me, I don't know. Maybe he was stupid enough to think I would be stupid enough to come back. That's probably what he thought.

After all, he couldn't think much of Earthlings if he wanted to make monkeys out of them. Or maybe our air wasn't right for him and he couldn't go out without a gas mask. Maybe he wanted me to get away. Maybe he was human, too, wanted me to find a way to stop this, to rescue him and... well, everyone else on Earth. Does he know who I am? Is he an alien, or isn't he? I began to wonder. He didn't look like an alien, but one never knows, does one? Do you?

I didn't light the cigarette. I stuffed it back in my pocket and ran. I looked back. He wasn't behind me. I slowed to a fast walk, weaving through the throng of people ambling along the walkway. I couldn't see him. But, of course, he didn't have to come after me, they had my number, my electromagnetic energy pattern—something. They could probably find me whenever they wanted to. Did he want me to get away? Obviously, he did not let very many other people get away, judging from the rows and rows of "transformed" humans. I still didn't know who I was, but I was getting an inkling that at least others knew I was somebody. Maybe he knew I was "somebody." Someone who might be able to stop the aliens. But I didn't have a clue how to stop them.

I stopped and looked around. I was in a place like an indoor mall, the dark wood of the place I had been in the forties predominated, wooden ramps and boardwalks along the shop fronts. A young woman was passing by with her mother. She said to me, "You've got some great shoes on, ha-ha." I looked at my feet. I was barefoot! She said to her mother, "That woman has been a ballerina. Look at her second toe, it's bent from dancing on her toes."

Her mother's eyes widened as she looked at my feet. "She has Morgan's Toe!" (The second toe is longer than the big toe.) She looked up at my face. Her mouth hung

open. She looked almost awestruck. I must look like a
maniac escaping from an asylum. Was I some kind of
freak? My second toe is longer than my big toe. It did
make it hard for toe dancing. "You'll have to cut them
off at the top joint if you want to continue dancing," my
mother had said. No thanks, Mom. I guess my toe dancing days are over. I didn't know my toes had a name.
Morgan's Toe—a genetic mutation!

"What does it mean?" I asked the woman.

"I read somewhere it makes one fleet of foot."

Great. Just what I needed to run from these aliens. I
hurried on. "Wait!" the woman called. "I want to talk to
you!" Why does she want to talk to me, a mutant–toed
ex–ballerina? Is it the DNA thing? Are my toes a sign
of something? Am I marked? Are people on the lookout
for me, to recognize me by my toes? Does she report to
the transformer man? I am beginning to get paranoid.
Beginning to? Who has more right at this moment to feel
paranoid than I? I really do have someone after me. I
wish I had some shoes. I don't know where the hell they
went. All this time, I sort of know what's going on, but I
sort of don't. I feel like a stranger here. What is, or was
my life? Where and when is this place? I can't remember, I can't remember enough to know who I am. Is there
engineered DNA hidden in me? DO YOU KNOW WHAT
I'M TALKING ABOUT? Am I some kind of messenger?

I keep going. I don't know who is safe to talk to in this
strange northern place. Somewhere north of San Francisco. Seattle? I seem to know how far away San Francisco is, even though I don't know where I am—not too
far, but much too far to walk, especially without shoes.
I would walk anyway, if I had to. Anything to get home.
The people seem nice enough, a bit vapid looking, a little
mindless. Still, I don't know who to trust, so I don't ask.

I haven't had time to think about what has happened,
how I got from the nineties to the forties and back again
to... when? Am I in the present? What exactly is the
present? Isn't is two thousand something? Can't tell. It
does seem different. I feel that I am in a future time. I

don't see cars on the street. I don't see a street. I think I'm on a sidewalk outdoors, but I really don't see the street. There are shops and an overhanging roof, but everything is very close. I can't see a street or the sky.

I keep walking. I go by a "residential" place. Like a day room, a living room. A couple of people are sitting in it. In their bathrobes. A large picture window on one side of the room. Trees and grass can be seen through the window in a courtyard. Looks normal. I step inside the room, look around briefly, then I go back out the door. A woman is after me, a psychiatrist, I think. How do I know that? She says, "You're not going anywhere. You get back in here, Christina!" I insist I don't belong there and I run away. That is my name, though. That much I know. How did she know? I've never seen her before. She must be one of them, the aliens. I'm not staying here!

Looking all around, I run down the walkway. The walkway is at a slight incline. There seems to be no outside, no way out of this strange place. All the time I am expecting them to come for me. Somehow I wind up near the transformation place again, but I don't recognize it in the moment. Finally, I see the outdoors, I think. Off the sidewalk, a grassy area. Trees on either side, framing the sky. A clear, night sky with a huge full moon, golden colored. It seems much larger than normal.

Then a space ship comes up into view and blasts the large apartment building across the street and turns it into rubble. "Oh my God!" I blink and look again. The building is still there as if nothing has happened to it. I don't understand. I turn away. I see a little lily pond up against the building in front of which I am standing. A father is standing there with his little boy. He is pointing up to the sky. A white crescent moon, much smaller than the one I saw a moment ago, is in the blue sky. The father is pointing to the crescent moon and saying, "Look, son. That's the sky moon."

I am totally perplexed. I just saw a full moon in the opposite direction, in the night sky, and a building that was destroyed, then not destroyed. I say, "Sky Moon?

What is that?"

A woman next to me says, "That's what we call the real, natural moon." She points to the big, full golden moon. "That's a hologram. We like to be entertained, so they put holographic scenes and movies everywhere."

"Who is 'they'?"

She shrugs her shoulders. "You know."

"How do they put movies everywhere?"

She shrugs again. She looks away, lost in thought, or a memory.

I wondered if the transformation thing was just pretend, part of the entertainment and wasn't really happening. Maybe I was experiencing one of their movies. Or maybe I'm engaging in some wishful thinking. I look again towards the building that I thought had been destroyed. Just for a split second, I thought the building looked transparent, and behind it a pile of smoking rubble. I blinked and it looked completely solid again. I can't decide what is real.

I still can't see any way out of the place. So I ask a woman, "How do I get out of here?" She points to the bus which is suddenly right there. I get on the bus. It doesn't have walls on the sides. Why not? Because it's all underground, goes slow, like a zoo tram. It seems to be night in this place. Always night, except for the scene of moons and the view out the window of the residential place. Maybe that view wasn't real, either.

The bus takes me to San Francisco and I get off the bus. It is night. It is quiet. There is not a soul around, not a person, not an animal, not a plant. I was so happy to be there, I didn't notice at first the utter silence of the cool night. No matter what hour of the night it was, there should be someone, some car, some cat, some light in a window. Nothing. I don't really notice at the time. I just think, I am out of that nightmare and although still a long way from home, too far to walk, I can call someone to come and get me. I would even walk home if I had to.

I want to call John the journalist to help me figure out what is going on, but I don't know how to reach him. How

do I get out of this nightmare! (It was after this dream
that I decided to write you.)

Suddenly in my mind it is black and these red numbers
and symbols are flashing past, the last one I see is the
Indian good luck symbol, similar to the Nazi swastika. At
first I think it is because the aliens are permanently imbedded in my mind now and know where I am. Are they
trying to program me? Then I realize it is their number
I've got. I am receiving their transmissions to aliens, it is
not them trying to transmit programming to me. However,
maybe someone is transmitting to me. Would I know the
difference? I certainly don't have any experience in this.
How can I decipher their transmissions? I am waking in
my bed as this is going on.

Then I think, this is the end of the movie? It is like that
number thing that goes on at the end of old movies, but
it's not usually in red. Why is this red, why are they so
large? Are there messages in those old movie reels?
Why do I feel like the receiving mechanism, the screen,
or the computer rather than just watching it? So, I must
have been dreaming, but this dream seemed as real as
life, perhaps more so. Well, it was a great dream, I think,
can make a great movie! I just check myself to make
sure I am still in my bathrobe and pajamas and haven't
been anywhere. I get up to get paper, pencil, and coffee
at 4:00 AM to write it down. Why do my feet and ankles
ache as if I've been walking or running all day?

I rub my feet. Now I have dirt on my hands. Why are
my feet so dirty? I showered before I went to bed!

What did John (you) write? Why couldn't I see it there?
In the dream, I felt I had met this John (you) before,
before the forties, even. Like we had always known each
other. Would I meet him again? Wait, it was only a dream,
I tell myself. You've never ever met this guy. He's just a
figure in a dream.

Why did I feel it imperative to get to the bottom of this
dream? What year did I meet him in the library? Why
did it have the same underground feeling of the rest of
the dream? Always falling in love with Jews? What did

this mean? Why am I even thinking about these stupid
dreams? Is it just an obsession I can't shake?

I draw some of the symbols I saw. They mean absolutely nothing to me. How can I find out what they mean?
The dirty feet bother me a lot. I had taken a shower
before I went to bed, so how did they get so dirty in bed?
I sit on the edge of the tub and wash my feet. Maybe it
wasn't a dream. Maybe I was seeing the future. Strange
symbols are flashing through my head again. I can't shut
them off. They go on and on for at least fifteen minutes.
Then they are gone and I am left here without answers.
Can you help me decipher these symbols? I've got to
know what they mean.

Please write or come visit me. They won't tell me what
the visiting hours are. I used to sit around waiting for
my boyfriend, or any friend, to come visit. I was upset
when no one showed. Somehow they've wiped my prior
knowledge of visiting hours out of my mind. Or they don't
give me visiting hours. When you come, don't tell them
you're a reporter. Make something up. Cousin, brother,
boyfriend, whatever. I won't bother you again if I don't
hear from you.
Christina

John's mind was totally scrambled. He tried to think about what
he had just read. *The ravings of a lunatic. Too bad such a beautiful
woman's mind was ruined. What a waste.* On the other hand, did
she just send him a plot for a movie? It was mind-boggling. Here
was a woman with more creative imagination in her little finger
than he had had in his whole life, and she didn't even know it was
her imagination so she couldn't use it to her advantage. *Maybe I
should go see her. Are you out of your mind, too, Davis? Get a grip.
No way would I want to get mixed up with her, even for a film. She's
already making me crazy!*

He tried earnestly to go on with his everyday life, but she kept
popping into his mind, especially at night when he was trying to
sleep. But he was determined not to succumb to his curiosity. She
hadn't written again for nearly two weeks, so maybe she'd given up.

2

The very next day there was another letter waiting for him at the office. He cringed when he saw it. Part of him wanted to put the letter back in the mail slot and leave it there forever, but another part of him was stronger and carried it to his desk.

November 29th

Dear John,

Happy Thanksgiving. I hope you have something to be thankful for. I have very little reason to be thankful. They appointed a new psychiatrist for me who is totally uninterested in anything I have to say. He just upped my dosage. But I manage to skip a pill here and there, so I won't be a total zombie. I can't believe they give people this mind-deadening stuff and think it's better to sit around like a zombie rather than be a screaming lunatic. Believe me, screaming is preferable to feeling dead.

I know I said I wouldn't write again if I didn't hear from you. I lied. I wish you'd check out the possibilities of inserting engineered genes into people, or at least into embryos. They don't let me do any research, or read any books. I'm supposed to rest and take it easy and weave baskets or something, and scrub the floor for therapy. Ha!

Listen! What I told you is the truth. If I tell you I'm thirty years old in my present incarnation, beautiful, sexy, and highly intelligent, then will you come to see me? You probably don't believe that, either, but really, that was my picture I sent you.

I remember another dream that may explain why I can receive their transmissions. In the dream, I am in the house where I grew up. We are outside in the front yard. It is a mild summer night. The stars are shimmering in the sky. Suddenly, a UFO appears in the sky. It is quite close. I can see the windows in it. It is shaped like the one in my more recent dream, except it is only like one half of the recent one. I go in the house.

The house was filled with party-like decorations—balloons, streamers, but not the normal kind. Weird, futuristic-looking decorations. They seemed to shimmer with their own light. There were closets full of new clothes. I was hoping they were for me. I was afraid there wouldn't be any for me, I would be left out. I looked in one closet of beautiful clothes and someone said those were for someone else. I didn't see anyone in the room. I just heard a voice. But then the voice said, "Here's your closet. Those are yours." They had selected clothes to suit each person perfectly. Different clothes for different occasions. I didn't get a very good look. Most of the clothes were ordinary. But there was one beautiful dress I got a good look at. I was sort of honored they thought so highly of me as to give me this perfect dress. It was very unusual. Sort of gypsy-like with modern style. It was perfect for me. Then a silver metal mandala was imprinted in my brain. It, too, was beautiful, and I felt in that moment that I had been touched by God, I felt the beauty and divinity of God, even though I knew an alien was responsible for the decorations, the dress, and the mandala in my brain. I went back outside, but the spaceship was gone. Was this mandala the receiver for the transmissions?

Write back, damn it!

Frustrated by the whole thing, John crushed the letter up in a ball in his hand and threw it in the trash with a vengeance. A minute later he took it out and smoothed it out and stuffed it in a drawer. He had an idea that maybe he could try to work her story into a screenplay without ever contacting her. He did not want to have anything to do with her.

Two days before Christmas John drove down to San Diego to visit his parents for a week. He began to feel relaxed, not plagued by thoughts of Christina and her story. He ate great home-cooked meals and played golf with his dad. He felt safer. He slept better. He drove back home on New Year's Day.

He tried off and on to get started on a screenplay based on Christina's story, but he couldn't get a good angle on it. He would need more information, he would need to know more about her to make it work. She wasn't writing any more and he wasn't going to contact her, so that was the end of that. He shelved the project and went on with his life. Day by day he thought about it less. By the time February rolled around, he hardly thought of it at all. Then one day, another one of those letters was waiting for him at the office.

February something

Dear John:

You haven't heard from me since November (at least I don't remember writing). The nurse saw a letter I was writing to you and she took it away. (The brother of my one and only friend here has been sneaking these letters out for me.) I have been heavily dosed ever since. They have lightened up now, because I've led them to believe I can't remember what I was doing or thinking before. They are partly right. There's a lot of my life I can't remember, but I think the mandala in my brain has preserved the important memories, the necessary ones to complete my mission. Of course, I can't remember who gave me this mission, if anyone did.

So many things have happened to me, so many weird dreams, weird experiences, ever since I can remember. Six years old, the most bizarre and telling dream. My life was being ruined by degrees. (Yes, I had a life once, although I no longer remember much about it.) I got so stressed out, I had to tell someone, get some help. I couldn't take not knowing what was reality and what was not. I went to a psychiatrist. Guess what happened after I spilled my guts about everything. Yep! Here I am at the Funny Farm.

The first dream I told you about was only one of many. I think the events I told you about are going to happen in the future. The aliens kidnapping, transforming us. Bombing our cities. How it will happen, I'm not sure you can handle the truth. Are you Jewish? It might help. If anyone is to listen, to hold a shred of belief, he will probably have to be Jewish, or maybe an atheist, because... just because.

Very tired. Losing it again. They forced me to take a pill. Until today, I'd been very good at hiding them.

Please come. Help me. Help the world.

Christina Markham

P.S. Room 213. The place is called Forest Vale. It's off of Occidental Road, in the forest. In a ravine with a little narrow bridge.

"So that's why she hasn't written," he said aloud. All the old feelings, the tightness in the gut, the thoughts swimming around her story, returned in full force. He felt compelled to meet her, see if he could get more of the story, more of her character. So, on the morning of February 14th John took his SUV out of the garage and headed north across the Golden Gate Bridge. It was a rare sunny day for that time of year, although a chilly wind was blowing some scattered clouds across the sky.

It wasn't easy to find the place. After traveling main roads for a while, he turned onto a narrow road which twisted and turned dangerously. John felt he was in an unending cave of giant redwood trees and thick undergrowth. He could hear a winter creek rushing very near, but he could not see it.

He half expected to see gnomes or trolls peering out from the bushes, but he didn't. What he did see suddenly was a deer which bolted out from the trees right in front of his car and then bounded to the other side of the road before he could even move his foot to slam on the brakes. Luck was with him that day, otherwise, he and the deer would probably both be dead.

Finally, he arrived at a sign which read "Forest Vale" with an arrow pointing downwards. He turned off slowly. The one-lane blacktop road ran steeply down to the bottom of a ravine, traversed by a winter creek now full of gushing water. He wondered if this was the right road as he drove across a narrow, questionable wooden bridge, and finally came to a clearing of sorts. The face of a concrete building was visible under a thick covering of green ivy. It reminded him of a military bunker. He didn't like the feel of the place at all. It didn't seem like the sort of place a mental or emotional disorder could be cured—more likely to cause one, he thought.

John parked his car and got out. Strangely, there were no other cars in the visitor parking area. He looked up through the treetops to see a glint of sunlight. *At least the sun is shining somewhere.*

Feeling more than a little unwelcome, he approached the building cautiously. A small sign by the door read "Forest Vale." The automatic door opened as he stepped in front of it. Inside, the walls were dull tan or gray, he couldn't tell which. He approached the information counter, but there was no one behind it. Apparently they weren't expecting visitors.

He saw the stairs, climbed them to the second floor. Some doors were open, others were closed. The room numbers were on the doors. Some had name labels in plastic slots. Some slots were empty. He followed the numbers until he came to Room 213. There was no name. The door was closed. He knocked gently. He listened. He could hear nothing. He knocked a little louder, still no sound. Gently he turned the knob and opened the door a little and peered in. She was sitting at a little desk, writing intently. John stepped into the room. She didn't notice him.

He stood there for a moment, gazing awestruck at her winsome beauty. A few strands of her long dark hair had strayed over one eye. She couldn't possibly be over thirty, much less sixty something.

"Christina?"

Startled, she fumbled with her papers and covered up her writing. She stood up and stared at John. "You came!"

John smiled and walked toward her, extending his hand. "John Davis."

"Hi." Christina shook his hand, brushed her hair back and somewhat nervously straightened her dress. "Do they know you're here?"

"There wasn't anyone downstairs, so I just came on up."

"It's just as well," she said. "I have a feeling they wouldn't have let you see me."

"Why not?"

"I don't know. I never get any visitors. They won't tell me when visiting hours are. If I talk too long to other patients, they hustle one of us off on some pretense or other. They treat me as if I'm a child, a mindless one at that." Christina looked toward the door, then went over and closed it softly. "I don't want them to make you leave before we've had a chance to talk. If we keep our voices down, maybe you can stay awhile. What time is it?"

John glanced at his watch. "Ten-ten."

"What day is it?"

"It's the fourteenth. Don't they let you have a watch, tell you what day it is?"

She shook her head. "They took my watch and anything else they think I could conceivably hurt myself with. A bell rings for meals. I have to ask if I want to know the date. Is it February?"

"Yeah. February. The fourteenth. Valentine's Day."

"Valentine's Day? It seems like years since I had someone to share Valentine's Day with." Christina looked around the room. "Sorry. Not much room to sit." She motioned to the edge of the bed and sat down. He sat down on the bed, too, at a non-threatening distance, one leg akimbo to sit sideways, facing her.

"So you were born in 1947? You're extremely well preserved. Were you in suspended animation or something for thirty years?"

Christina laughed. "Not to my knowledge. I was born in forty-seven, but that was my previous incarnation. I must have died rather young, but I don't remember my death."

"When I saw your picture," John said, "I thought you looked familiar. I think I've seen you somewhere before."

"So you remember your past life, too?"

"No, in this life. A party, a bar, a restaurant. Somewhere."

"Well, I've never seen you in this life, except on TV once. And then, I knew I'd met you before. Because of what I wrote you about. Do you believe what I wrote you about?"

"I believe you had those dreams. I don't know what they mean. I can't verify the truth or falsity of them."

Christina stood up, walked over to the window, looked out. "Then why did you come?"

"Your letters, your picture, intrigued me. I wanted to know more about you, about the dreams."

She looked out the window again. "Is that your car down there?"

John got up, looked out the window. "Yeah."

She turned to him. "I've got to get out of here. Take me with you!"

"Uh… you're not locked up. The front door is unlocked. Your room door is unlocked. Why haven't you already left?"

"I tried once. I didn't get very far. They came after me. Told me there were mountain lions out there, I have to stay inside. I think they've imbedded a tracking chip in me. I don't know how else they found me."

"If that's the case, what good will it do if you go now? If they can track you, you won't get very far. And then they would know who I am, and would prevent us from connecting again. Anyway, someone probably just saw you leave. It's hard to believe they'd go to the trouble to imbed some electronic device when they don't believe your story."

Christina responded angrily. "It's not a story! What I have to say is the truth! There's something horrible going on, and no one but me seems to know about it!"

He took her hand, patted it gently. "I didn't mean it that way. I mean they would think of it as a story, as something you made up. It's not easy to believe that something so ominous is going on, or will go on. I'm keeping an open mind. I just want to know more."

"There's someone looking at your car. Now they're going towards the building. You'd better get out of here. Try not to let them see you! There's another door on the side. Turn left out my door. End of the hall, downstairs. It's right there. It might have an alarm, though."

"Don't worry. I'll figure it out." He opened the door, looked out into the hall, then stepped out. "Wait!" She grabbed the papers from the desk, thrust them into his hands.

She watched him as he walked quickly down the hall and disappeared down the stairs.

John saw no one as he walked to his car, but he felt eyes watching his back. The place was just too eerie. He tried to shrug it off. He heard a deep growling sound—like purring, but from something much bigger than a house cat. Mountain lion? *Why the hell would anyone build a sanitarium out here in the wild?* He got in his car quickly and got out of there as fast as he could. *I'm never coming back here,* he thought, but he knew he'd have to. Compelled to... that woman. *Crazy. Or is she? Funny how she can act so rational... living in another reality.*

3

Once he was out of there and back to civilization, John stopped for a cup of coffee. Strong and black. He sat down at a table in the corner. Some sort of haze had settled over his mind out there in the woods and he wanted to reclaim his brain. Wake it up. He sat down and took out the now wadded papers of Christina's that he had stuffed in his pocket in his... escape. That's what he felt, that he had escaped something unnameable, some unknown, yet strongly felt threat. Maybe it was just his escape from a crazy but very attractive woman. She hadn't escaped. She was stuck in it. All her own doing. She had allowed herself to fall into a dream, a nightmare, and now she couldn't get out of it. He had thought he was just following up a story, but now he felt he was becoming enmeshed in it, sucked in. Did he really escape just because he drove away? He straightened out the papers. *I should throw them away. Not read anything from her ever again.* He looked at the trash can by the door, but his body wouldn't move to get up and take the papers over there. He looked down at the first page.

February something

Dear John, again —
I still haven't heard from you. I can tell you plenty more, but I have to be careful how much I reveal at once, or I might totally scare you off. I have not received any of my letters back from the post office, so I assume you are getting the letters. And... I think they have piqued your interest. Otherwise, after the first or second letter they would have come back refused. Am I right? Maybe not. Maybe they are coming back to the

hospital and being intercepted. Or, maybe you just throw them away.

I went to a psychiatrist because I couldn't feel my self. I didn't feel like anybody. Here's how it was to be on the outside of me—

My psychiatrist says, "You don't know who you are!" Is he angry? It seems a crime to not know. I have a name. I have a body. I have a checking account and credit cards with my name on them. My psychiatrist was right. I didn't know who I was. I didn't feel like "me."

I feel I have to say something to him, pretend I have an answer. "I'm a child of God," I say in sheepish, weak defense.

"Yes, you are," he says, "but…" That's all he said about it. He seemed frustrated.

I searched for me from the beginning. I kept going back, back, to my childhood, to my birth, before my birth, another life, another time. I know there is no end, no real death. There is no beginning and there will be no end. But somewhere, I must start with this tale of my life, or my lives.

From there, which branch shall I take back to the past? How far? Which story? Much the same story is played over and over again. Jealous husbands, jealous wives. Heroes and scoundrels, one and the same. Beautiful women, talented women, mistresses and wives. Dying for a cause, civil war, rebellion, lost horses, lost homesteads, lost castles, lost crowns. Lost minds. Kings and queens, Jesus, Noah. My name— Christina—is this a clue to who I am? Jesus Christ? Returned to save the world from the alien menace?

I dream that I am in heaven and there are some people there with me. This life has all been planned in advance. I feel their love. I seem to have come home. I am really Jesus Christ, returned to save the world. Yet I'm not, or don't appear to be. I look in the mirror. I'm in the same female body, but inside I'm Jesus. My face suddenly looks like a man. It's like I forgot who I was. I had amnesia for 1,000 years. Now I know I am Jesus. I am shocked. How can this be? I don't know what to say to anyone the following morning. I go out to the co-op market. I don't usually shop there. I just want to get out of the house before I die of insanity. I wear my man's tweed sport coat, jeans and black oxfords. And I feel like a man. I AM Jesus, awakened in the 21st Century. I am totally centered.

There is none of my usual nervousness or anxiety of being in public. It is a charming little store. There is all manner of art which my children have made. I look at a peach-colored glass dish. The color swirls through clear glass. Sand sparkles in little rivulets that run through the color. It is a beautiful wonder what this artist has wrought. I turn around and come face to face with a birthday card that says, "Happy Birthday on your first day of life." I go to the supermarket where I usually shop. I am standing in line at the quick-check counter. I am surrounded by mylar balloons that shout "Happy Birthday!" and "It's a boy!" They weren't there yesterday!

So now you perhaps think you know why they put me in here. I don't know why. There are two possibilities. Either I am Jesus, here to save the world from the aliens, and they want to stop me, or I am crazy. More dreams and memories began to

This must be where I walked in, John thought. *I don't quite see how she can think it means she's Christ. What an imagination! Yeah, I know why they put her in there. She's crazy. But it's looking more and more like movie material. Probably be a mess, though, if I get involved, even on a business level, with a crazy woman. As to being involved any other way, avoiding that could be a problem, she is so...* John shook his head. *I had no idea her delusions ran so deep.* He put off contacting her again—indefinitely.

—∿∿—

Christina, however, did not stop contacting him. Soon after, she sent some undated, unsigned handwritten notes. He could tell, of course, they were from her by the content, as well as the handwriting.

*More memories of strange experiences and dreams begin to
surface. I remembered an inexplicable experience, which I had
long since put out of my mind. The night of January 20th I
felt very strange. I was reading Revelations. I am an obsessive
mystery solver. It doesn't matter whether I can solve it or not, I
just keep digging. I was trying to understand Revelations. And
then a possibility hit me… The image of the beast—hologram?
The time is ripe. Who is the evil leader, the 666 antichrist?*

*GGG handwritten looks similar to 666. (I recently learned
that an ancient Greek numerical system using letters of the
Greek alphabet use the lower case "G" letter. Revelations was
written in Greek. My great-great grandfather Markham. His
social security number started with 666. The mark of the
ham—the "mark of the beast"?*

*The beast and the image of the beast who could be made to
walk and talk. Television? A movie, a hologram? A beast who
has technology at his fingertips, who promises to bring heaven
to earth, make the desert bloom. Your every dream fulfilled.
But on the other side of that…*

An earthling tool of the aliens? The antichrist?

*His great-great-grandfather the same as mine? Are my
"Morgan's" toes the mark? I was born in the Chinese Year of
the Pig. Ridiculous. I am not the beast, but perhaps I have
been marked for something. Could the beast be one of my
distant relatives?*

*The theory that Jesus survived the crucifixion and went to
live in France with Mary Magdalene and had children. He
said they would have had descendants, but nobody knows who
they are. The psychiatrist had said to me, "You don't know who
you are!" The theory that one daughter went with Mary—the
other children could have been grown already. She was still
small and needed her mother.*

*Maybe genetic memory is what I've got. Genetic memory of
being Jesus, because I am his descendant. The man who wants*

to rule the world—the antichrist. He is also a descendant of Jesus, but he is not aware of it.

So, as the photons are still connected when split, maybe I am connected to this antichrist. Deep down I know what he is up to. Genetic memory is one thing, but how do you explain the transmissions—maybe the same way—genetic memory. This is more important if we leave out the aliens.

Many sightings of UFO, angels, etc., could be holograms. Well, what about holograms all over the world or even just in the US? Is this what they're planning? I don't see how anyone, even an Israeli, outside our government, could do that. Maybe aliens will set someone up as their puppet. How are they going to locate just the right earthling to play Jesus on the ground. Or does an alien play the part?

Holograms projected from satellites while his armies take out the entire United States and Western Europe. Only a nonbeliever could fathom the deception of the anti-Christ.

Those who had figured out what is going on, such as I, are among the first that they try to transform.

"I'll have my angels prepare things so you can have a heaven on earth," the Beast says.

Thanks for nothing! Now lock your bathroom door, people. You never know when they are going to show up. (like it says in the Bible--look it up).

What kind of Chronicles was John writing in the forties???

She was beginning to get to him, making him wonder… were there such Chronicles written by a John in the forties? *What the hell. I might as well check it out.*

4

Back home, John logged into the newspaper archives. He searched year after year until he came to February 1946. That was where he found the article "Chronicles," by-line John Davis! It chronicled the history of the Jews and their contributions to the history of the world. He could find nothing unusual about it, except for one little thing. The name of the reporter. His name! *Just a coincidence.* As unbothered as he wanted to feel about it, John was a little jolted by the coincidence.

He seemed to have little power over his growing obsession with the idea of making her story into a screenplay. On his next day off, he headed north again to see Christina. Even though it was early March and the sun was shining brightly other places, the forest seemed as dark and forbidding as ever. *Why am I here, what am I doing?* Even so, he got out of his car and entered the building.

There was someone at the counter this time, but her back was turned. Not knowing if he would be welcome, John moved stealthily across the lobby, up the stairs and down the hall to Christina's room. As he raised his fist to knock, the door opened. There was Christina, her face inches from his.

"I heard your car pull up. I knew it was you."

John smiled, his mind scrambled. She was too close to him. He wanted to run, but seemed frozen in place. Christina opened the door, and said, "Well, don't just stand there. Come in."

He still couldn't think of anything to say. She put her hand on his arm and propelled him gently into the room. "I'm so glad you came. Now please, please get me out of here. I can't take it another day. I want a normal life, no matter who I am, or was in the past. I'm not dangerous. I wouldn't make any scenes in public or get you in trouble somehow."

John laughed in spite of the seriousness of her plea.

"You think it's funny? Would you want to be cooped up in this place, people watching you like a hawk all the time?"

Finally, John found some words. "No. I was only laughing at your audacity to think someone who hardly knows you would just whisk you away from here without the hospital's OK. And I was laughing at myself for considering doing it."

"Well? Will you? We could just try walking out. If they say anything, we're just walking around."

"Where will you go once you're out of here? I don't think I can have you staying at my place."

Christina laughed. "I'm not exactly broke. I have a home and a large trust fund, unless they found a way to steal it all from me."

"Oh. Well, uh…" John couldn't find any more excuses.

"The only thing is, I don't want to stay at my house, because they might look for me there. I've had plenty of time on my hands to make a plan. You rent a house for me in your name. I'll give you the rent money and you pay the rent. Okay?"

"I… I don't think it's a good idea."

"Why not? Just get me out of here. Just take me home so I can get my ATM card and get some money. You won't have to see me again after that!"

John couldn't find the word "no," or any words at all. Christina fished some papers out from their hiding place in her closet and stuffed them in his jacket pocket. Then she took him by the arm and they walked out of her room.

"If anyone sees us, just act natural, like you're just visiting, and you think you have a right to be here."

"Okay."

The woman at the counter turned around and noticed them right away. "Christina! What are you doing? Who is that?" To John she said, "You didn't sign in!" She came out from behind the counter.

Christina smiled blissfully. "This is my cousin George. He found out I was here and came to visit. Isn't it wonderful? I finally have a visitor. You know, I feel so much better and more present just knowing someone cares."

"Well, maybe it's okay, Christina, but if you start acting up, I'll have to report it. Where are you going? You're not supposed to leave the grounds."

John spoke up. "We're just going to get a little fresh air."

The woman stepped to block their way from the front door. She pointed down a hallway. "The patients' patio is that way, but first you'll have to sign in."

John obliged her and signed in as George Markham. Then they feigned a leisurely stroll down the hall to the patio.

The first thing John looked at was the locked gate and the four-foot high lattice fencing. Not high security at least, he thought. There was no one else on the patio. No one was watching from the door.

"Well, Cousin George," she teased, "what now?"

"If we put a chair by the fence, can you climb over?"

"Of course." She smiled. "You may think I'm feeble-minded, but I'm certainly not feeble-bodied." They climbed over the fence and slunk stealthily to the side of John's car farthest away from the entrance door. John saw the woman from the lobby run out from the entrance towards them, waving her hand. Christina climbed over the gear shift console to the passenger seat and John got in, key in hand. The tires squealed as he floored the gas. They left the woman glaring after them in the parking lot.

Christina was bouncing in her seat like a child. "We did it! We did it! Hooray!"

John was less excited. "Yeah, we made it." *Now what,* he was wondering. Ever since that first letter, she had seemed somewhat unreal to him. He had felt like a character in a movie. Things had suddenly turned real, with her sitting in his car beside him, and he wasn't sure he liked it at all. He only wanted to get rid of her, drop her off somewhere.

"How do we get to your place?"

"I'm not sure, at least not from here. But it's in Marin. Larkspur. If you can get me to town, I can direct you from there. "Did you know they scanned my brain?"

John looked over at her. "No. I know very little about you."

"Well, they did. They said they found an anomaly. An unusual structure in one little place in my brain. Not metal, if you're thinking one of those implants people claim they got from aliens. Maybe it is an alien implant, but of a biological nature. They thought it had messed up my thinking. They wanted to operate and remove it, but I might have permanent brain damage. So I said absolutely not."

"So they didn't operate?"

"No, not yet anyway. They said they would wait and see, but I think they've been planning all along to try to remove it eventually. That's one reason I wanted to get out of there as soon as possible. You can't trust these people who always think they know best."

John thought for a moment. "I guess it really comes down to can you live with the way you are, and if the alternative is worse than that."

"Yes."

"Yes what?"

"Yes I can live with the way I am, and I think the alternative would be worse." Christina put her seat back and closed her eyes. She drifted off to sleep.

After a little while, they arrived in Larkspur and John shook her gently on the shoulder. "We're in Larkspur now." She gave him directions and he drove her home.

Christina's house was on a narrow street that wound up a hill. It was a large white Victorian with lots of gingerbread.

"What did you do to rate such a big, beautiful house all your own?" he asked as he got out of the car. Christina looked around for watchers before she got out. She walked warily up to the house, looking up and down the street, as well as behind her.

"Nothing, except be born," Christina replied. "It was my parents' home. I grew up here. I inherited it when they died. I don't have a key, but I've hidden one here." She dug around in a planter until she found it. She brushed the dirt off her hands and the key, then she pushed the buttons on the keypad for the alarm system, turned the key and opened the door. She turned on the light in the foyer.

"Why's the electricity's still on when you've been away so long?"

"Automatic bill pay. Lucky for me. I'd be a good endorsement for the service." She laughed. 'Even if you're locked up for months, your bills go on being paid.'"

John laughed, too. He liked her ability to maintain a sense of humor in adversity.

"I have a post office box—a good thing, or my mail would be all over the street by now."

"Yeah," John laughed again. "Quite a place, Christina. And now that I got you here, I'm going to say goodbye."

"Do you think you could do one more little thing and take me to pick up my mail? I think there's going to be too much for me to carry on foot."

"Don't you have a car?"

"I left it at my psychiatrist's office months ago, when they came and got me. Either my psychiatrist's driving around in it or it was towed away and sold at auction."

"All right, but after that, I've got to go."

"Just let me find an ATM card, and then I'll be ready."

John wandered down the hall. A library with walls of books drew him in. He thumbed through a few books while he waited. Books about extraterrestrial encounters, science, New Age spirituality, history, voices from the other side and so on. Did all these books fuel her madness, or was she searching for some sanity in them? He turned away from the books and looked at the desk. A framed photo of a middle-aged couple sat near the computer. Her parents? What had happened to them? How was it that both of them were dead? Was it when they died that she lost her sense of reality? He noticed another photo on the wall, one with her parents, Christina, and two other young people. Her brother and sister?

At this point, Christina walked in, attired in a different, filmy, dreamy dress. She had put on some lipstick and mascara. If he had thought her desirable before, now he was totally captivated, standing there with his mouth hanging open, staring like an idiot.

"I haven't found my card yet. I know there's one around here somewhere." She moved to the desk, brushing his arm as she reached for the drawer. "Maybe it's in here."

A hint of exquisite expensive perfume hit him. Only a whiff, but the slightly sweet, vanilla essence just about melted him.

"Voila!" she exclaimed, holding up the card.

He shook off the enchantment as best he could and drove her to the post office. Christina had stacks of mail, mostly junk mail. John helped her sort it in the post office and throw the junk in the trash. He had recovered from his temporary insanity of wanting to follow her to the ends of the earth—and beyond, if necessary. He smiled and said, "Well, now. You don't have much to carry home if you walk."

Christina looked at him like a lost little girl. "But I don't have any food in the house. I have to do some shopping."

John shook his head slightly. He couldn't get out of this precarious situation yet. He couldn't desert a damsel in distress who didn't have anything to eat. "To the store then, but after that I'm leaving and you can carry on your weird life without me," he said just a little too harshly. Christina looked at him sadly. He wished she wouldn't look at him that way.

John pushed the cart up and down the aisles as Christina picked items from the shelves and put them in the cart. "I never thought grocery shopping could be so much fun, but after being locked up for so long, I love just walking up and down the aisles and looking at everything." She stopped in front of the deli counter. "It's lunch time. You must be hungry. How about if I get some sandwiches for us?"

John couldn't deny he was hungry, so he agreed.

He took her back to her place and carried the groceries into the kitchen. He helped her put the groceries away. She took out a couple of plates and set out the sandwiches on them, along with deli pickles and fruit salad. She put them on the kitchen table along with a couple of bottles of sparkling mineral water.

They ate in silence for a few minutes. After John's hunger pangs abated, he dared to speak. "If it's not too traumatic for you to answer, can you tell me how it is that both of your parents have died?"

"They were killed in an auto accident, only I don't think it was an accident."

"What happened?"

"The brakes failed. There wasn't any brake fluid. Not like my father at all. He was always meticulous about keeping the cars serviced and running smoothly. The investigators found a trail of brake fluid leading up to the scene. It seems suspicious to me that it should have been leaking out."

"Did they determine why it had been leaking?"

"They couldn't tell. The car was badly burned." She put down her sandwich and got up from the table. She looked like she was going to cry. "I'm sorry, Christina. I guess I asked too many questions. I didn't mean to ruin your lunch. It's the damned reporter in me. I don't know when to stop."

"It's okay. I just don't think I'll ever get over it."

He got up and cleared the table. He wanted to put his arms around her, comfort her, but it was too risky. He wouldn't want to stop. Instead, he started rinsing the dishes and putting them in the dishwasher.

"What are you doing?"

"The dishes. It's the least I can do after ruining your lunch."

His ploy to lighten her mood worked. Christina smiled and shook her head. "Not necessary."

"Not on your part, maybe, but definitely on mine." He finished putting the dishes in the dishwasher and closed it up. "It's not full yet."

Christina laughed. "We'll have to work on filling it up later."

John came back to his senses when she said that. *She thinks I'm going to stay long enough to dirty more dishes.* "I'm sorry, but you'll have to do that on your own. I've got to go. I have a lot of work piling up at my office."

"Oh."

"I do have a job, you know."

"Of course, John. It's just that I don't feel safe here. They've got my address, and they might come looking for me."

"Who's they? The hospital? The aliens?"

"Maybe both."

"Look, Christina. I doubt any aliens are after you. And the hospital, well, I don't think they have a right to keep you. If they pick you up, I'll get a court order to release you."

"Don't you believe me about the aliens?"

"I'm a skeptic. Show me some proof, then I might believe you."

"So you think I'm crazy."

"I think you've been traumatized by your parents' deaths. It can happen to anyone. It doesn't mean you're crazy, at least not in the long term." He tried to appease her. "You have an active imagination. Something every writer desires, but very few have."

"I hate to admit it, but you're right about my imagination. Still, the things that happened to me were very real." She walked him to the door. "I've been thinking. I still believe they'll come for me. I can't stay in this house alone. I'll gladly pay you for the inconvenience if you would camp out here for a few days."

John opened the door. "I really don't think it's necessary, Christina."

"I don't care if you think it's necessary. It's necessary for me! I will be a nervous and sleepless wreck if I have to stay here alone." She grasped his arm gently but firmly and looked into his eyes pleadingly. "Please, I'm begging you. Please. I have a guest room." She smiled. "You'll be safe in there from me. You can lock the door."

"Well, how can I say no? I wouldn't want you to lose your beauty sleep and turn into an ugly hag overnight. I'll stay tonight, but right now I have to go into the office. Like I said, I've got work to do. I'll be back this evening." He started to go out the door, but she still held his arm.

"Wait. I'll write down the code for the alarm and give you a key. In the unlikely event I'm asleep when you get back." She wrote the code down and gave it and a key to him.

"See ya," John said hurrying out the door before some other excuse stopped him.

5

John made an appearance at his office, sat down at his desk and stared at his computer screen. He knew he had to finish an article for the next morning, but his mind wouldn't cooperate. All he could think of was Christina and how he was trapped into spending more time with her. Not just more time, but sleeping in the same house with her. Why was he so attracted to a psychotic? Was it the risk level? Was he crazy, too? Could she be dangerous? Did she have a gun? Would she use it on him if he tried to get away? Why didn't he just not go back to her house, ever? He felt like a fly in a spider web, or rather a black widow male spider, aware of a likely death if he mated, killed and eaten by the female, but powerless to resist. He knew he would succumb sooner or later, probably sooner.

She thought she might be Jesus? Or his descendent? No wonder she was locked up. The antichrist was coming, masquerading as Jesus? Suddenly, inspiration hit him. A scene played in his mind. "Yes! That's great! A scene for the screenplay!" John quickly thought up a working title and then started typing a rough draft of the scene feverishly.

Washington DC 08:30 EDT
The busy streets of Washington, DC. People are hurrying to work. Above the din of honking horns and jackhammers, something else is heard from above—a sound like a trumpet, at first almost inaudible, then growing in amplitude until a woman stops and looks up in the direction of the sound. Someone else stops and looks up. Another and another look up. A glowing light above the street grows lighter and brighter. Soon everyone is looking

up, their mouths gaping in disbelief at what they see.

A huge cloud with radiant light glowing from it has formed above them in what was a moment ago a relatively clear sky. Out of the light appears the glowing radiance of a man clothed in a white robe on a small cloud. He is surrounded by angels.

He speaks in a booming voice. "As it is written, the end is here and the Kingdom of God is at hand."

People are awestruck, mesmerized. Two people fall in a faint, or a heart attack, maybe. Many fall to their knees. "Oh my God!" one says, not in prayer but in astonishment. Then the cloud with Jesus descends slowly over the lawn near the White House.

Secret Service men and guards rush out to the scene. One by one, several people ascend into the light and disappear in the cloud. People gasp.

The glowing light increases to blinding intensity until Jesus and his angels cannot be seen for a moment, then as it dims again Jesus and several men can be seen on the ground.

The people stand back in awe. Even the Secret Service agents stand back. The guards maintain a stance of readiness with some difficulty.

Jesus walks up to one of the Secret Service agents, followed by twelve white-robed men.

"Take me to your leader. I wish to speak with him immediately."

"Who are you? Are you Jesus?"

"Thou sayest it."

"One minute," the agent says and puts his walkie-talkie to his ear, his eyes on Jesus.

"Would you keep me waiting?"

"Mr. President, Jesus Christ is here to see you... Yes, sir," the agent says into the phone. "Well, I think it might really be him, because he descended on a cloud from the sky."

Listening, then: No, sir. I'm not on anything. Hundreds of people saw him. He's got, uh, one, two three... twelve men in robes with him." He listens some more. "Yes, sir."

"Follow me," the agent says and starts to turn, but turns back with a sheepish grin, "I mean, come with me, Lord."

The twelve men follow Jesus. Two guards stop them with their rifles. "Agent Bender, do you want these men to wait here?"

"Yeah. Just uhhh...Jesus to see the President."

Jesus nods his head to the men. He smiles to the agent. "They are my apostles, my followers. However, it wouldn't be the first time I came before a king alone."

The agent smiles, too. "The President is not a king. He is elected by the people."

Jesus stares at him a moment. "I am aware of that, and everything else that occurs on this planet... Earth."

They walk toward the entrance, people kneeling to Jesus as he passes.

The President rushes in to the Oval Office, followed by his <secretary, aide, whatever.> "Get me someone on the phone, quick!"

"Who, Mr. President?"

"Damned if I know! The Pope or somebody. Some bible expert. The Pentagon, the Cabinet, uh...yeah, get me General Swarter."

The Secret Service agent steps in, followed by Jesus. The president turns to face Jesus, looks him in the eyes. "What is this? What's going on?"

"Don't you know? I thought you were a Christian. I've returned as I promised, and bringing the kingdom of God to earth. I would think you'd be joyful."

"Well, I am astounded. I don't know what to say." The President gestures to a chair. "Have a seat, Lord, and let's talk about it."

Jesus looks at the chair, and then at the President's chair behind the desk. He walks around the desk and seats himself in the President's chair. Still standing, the President stares at him in silence.

Jesus gestures to the chair the President had intended for him. "Have a seat, son. I want to talk to you." The President remains standing. "James...that is the name of my brother. Your name also. Do you think that is a coincidence?"

"I guess so. Lots of people are named James. Thousands, I'm sure. What are you going to do?"

"You already know, if you are one of my followers. You ARE a Christian, are you not?"

"Yes, I am."

"Well, then, I shouldn't have to explain, but I will anyway. I'm going to rule earth for a thousand years."

"When will the Resurrection take place?"

"Soon, but first there is much to do."

"Like what?"

Jesus looks up at the ceiling—and beyond, it seems. Then he looks back. "I shall require your dedicated service, as My Father has always required the service of men and women everywhere to do His holy work."

"I don't know exactly what you require of me yet, but I'll do my best to serve God."

"As I am one with the Father, and therefore also God, say you will serve ME."

"If you are God, then I have said it."

"You must disarm your nuclear weapons immediately. All nations with nuclear weapons must disarm them. Then, as quickly as possible you will dismantle them. They are too dangerous. There must be no more war of any kind. No more fighting amongst yourselves."

"As long as all the nations disarm, so will the United States of America, but some nations may not want to cooperate with you. Not everyone is a Christian. They don't all believe in you. Christians are a minority in the world."

"I will show myself to every person on earth. Then they will believe. There's a lot to do to bring Heaven to Earth. It must be done somewhat gradually. I don't want to cause the people a great shock at the changes I am bringing."

"What kind of changes?"

"Good changes, heavenly changes. A perfect life, blessed in all ways for everyone. But much of your present life, the good and the practical, these things can still go on. Worship, work, play. These things will simply be more enjoyable, and abundance shall flow for all people from God.

"I will speak to the United Nations. I want it broadcast on your televisions, radios, internet, around the world. Tonight."

"When I leave here, there will be people gathered outside who want to touch me. I want you to keep them at a distance. It would not do to have them mob me in their eagerness for my touch. I have many disciples and saints with me who can act in my behalf in such matters after the important matter of disarmament is taken care of."

"Excuse me for asking, but God is all powerful. Why doesn't He, or you, just disarm the weapons Himself?"

Jesus blinked his eyes several times, seeming somewhat perturbed. "Because... it is a final test to determine whether people are worthy of God and Heaven. They must be willing to trust and to obey Him... me, that is. I was speaking of the Father, but I am God also."

Jesus rose and walked out, the Secret Service agents with him. The crowd was being held back with some difficulty as Jesus walked to the place where he had

The phone rang. *So much for artistic endeavors. I'm always brought back to reality too soon.* It was Christina. "John! I'm scared. There's a prowler walking around outside my house. I looked out the window and saw him digging in my garbage can. He's looking for something."

"Probably food. What else would he be looking for?"

"I don't know. Evidence of some kind, or to make sure I'm me. Please come over right away."

"I can't leave yet. I'm still working. Did you call the police?"

"No! Do you think they'd take me seriously? They might take me back to the sanitarium! Please come over!"

The anxiety in her voice got to him. "I guess I can finish my article on my laptop and e-mail it in. I'll be there soon."

"Please hurry." Christina hung up.

John quickly saved the scene on the office computer, grabbed his jacket and his laptop and left.

Even though he had a key, John rang the doorbell. Christina must have been waiting near the door, because she opened it almost immediately. She took him by the arm, practically pulled him inside. "I'm so glad you're here! Now I'll be able to sleep tonight."

"Great," John said a little sarcastically. "Where's the prowler?"

"He's gone," I think."

"Good. I've got to finish my article now. I'm going right to my room. Please don't interrupt me unless it's an emergency."

"Okay. Do you want a cup of coffee or a sandwich?"

"Yeah."

"Yeah what?"

"Yeah both."

"I'll bring them up." She gave him a rather coy look. "I promise I won't otherwise disturb you until your article is finished."

"Thanks. Could you wait about half an hour? I want to finish it before I eat."

"Sure."

John went upstairs to his room and shut the door behind him. He looked for a lock on the door, but it was an old-fashioned door with a keyhole, and there was no key in it. He made a mental note to ask for a key.

He set up his laptop on a small antique roll-top desk painted white in the Victorian-style bedroom. The room was large but cozy due to the fireplace and warm wood tones of the other furniture, and the beautiful old quilt coverlet on the double bed.

He was well into his article by the time she knocked on the door and entered with a tray holding a sandwich, a slice of bakery cake, and coffee. She set the tray on a small table near the bay window and sat down in one of the two chairs by the table.

John came over and picked up the sandwich and coffee. He started back to the desk.

"You're not going to eat while you work? It's not good for your digestion."

Somewhat grudgingly, as if his mother were scolding him, John returned to the table and sat down. "I don't want any cake, but thanks for bringing it."

"I'll eat it then," she said, reaching for the fork. "How's your article going?"

"It's almost done. Just a few more sentences." He ate in silence, trying to think about his article while he ate. Thoughts of getting her in that bed across the room kept intruding on his mind. With the last bite in his mouth he took up his coffee and went back to the desk. Christina was still nibbling on the cake.

John finished his article and opened an e-mail window and addressed it. A thought of his screenplay scene distracted him and he decided to transfer the scene to his laptop so he logged in to his office computer and opened the scene document. At that moment, Christina came over and stood behind him. "Can I read it?" She leaned over him to peer at the screen. He didn't want her to see the screenplay scene, at least not until he could explain to her what he wanted to do. He quickly copied and pasted the scene to an e-mail and sent it to himself, and closed the document.

Unfortunately, without knowing it he had not sent the scene to himself. He had pasted it in the e-mail he meant for his article and sent it to the paper. More than that, his confused mind registered that he had sent in his article to the paper.

Very flustered now, he closed his article, thinking it was the scene he had written. He knocked his coffee cup off the desk. He stared at the pool of coffee on the carpet.

"Don't worry, John. It won't hurt anything. I'll get a towel."

John made it through the rest of the night without further mishap. In his eagerness to get out of Christina's house (read that, "Christina's web"), he arrived at his office early, a rare event. "Hey, John!"

"Hi, John!" various dedicated early arrivers greeted him. They stared at him quizzically. He nodded and kept going. *Why are they looking at me like that? It's not that unusual for me to be a little early.*

He soon found out the reason for the stares. The intercom buzzed before he could sit down. It was Alison, the editor-in-chief's secretary. He was being called on the carpet, for what, he hadn't the slightest idea.

He knocked lightly on the door and opened it. He had barely stepped into the room before Ross jumped out from behind his desk waving the morning paper in his hand. "What the hell is this? Are you crazy? I thought you had more sense than to write this crap that will inflame three quarters of our readers! We're gonna lose advertisers over this. We're gonna lose subscribers. We'll be the laughingstock of the news world! We might even get sued by people who have heart attacks over it!"

"What are you talking about? It's just the same stuff…"

"Bullshit! You made this bullshit up and tried to pass it off as news! It can't be true."

"It is true. It's a carefully researched, and if I say so myself, a well written account of the events."

"Ha! Like you have some White House informant that no one else has. The only other reporting about this is the flat denial of it by the Press Secretary, not to mention possible criminal charges against you and the paper for terrifying the public and causing civil unrest! The FBI is due here any minute to investigate your subversive activity! Then I suppose there'll be the NSA, the CIA, and every letter in the alphabet."

"I don't know what you're talking about, Ross. Let me see." He reached for the paper in Ross' hand. There in boldface type was the headline that would ruin his career forever as a journalist. "**THE SECOND COMING IS NOW!**"

"No. No. No! This is my screenplay! How did they get it? Somebody wants me fired! Someone who wants my job."

"It doesn't matter why! You ARE fired, no matter why, how, or who. We can't have you on the paper any more, and we'll have to recant your story and explain you're an idiot, and crazy as well. There's no telling what kind of trouble we're in for!"

The FBI. They'll be here soon to ruin the other parts of my life. I've got to get out of here NOW! "Just send me my paycheck." John turned and stormed out. He saw them, two FBI-looking guys coming toward him in the hall. He slowed down to what he hoped was a leisurely, non-guilty pace and nodded to them as he passed by. Now out of their sight, he took the stairs two at a time down to the parking garage. He had to slow down in the garage because two other FBI types were standing around there. His heart was racing, but he held himself to an even, normal pace on the long, long, walk of a hundred feet to his car.

Even so, they reached his car just as he slammed the door and turned on the ignition. He took off. He figured Ross would explain the error and they wouldn't throw him in prison—he hoped.

John drove past the Larkspur exit. He kept on driving. He wasn't in the mood to see Christina. He was blaming her for his loss of a job. He had hoped someday to be famous for his writing, not infamous. He'd never live it down, never get another job. He exited the freeway and headed out to Tomales Bay. Cloudy, cold, wind-whipped. The cold salt air stinging his face was the perfect remedy for his anger and despondency. He walked on the beach about a mile and back, just enough to feel totally alone in the world. The walk worked. The cold wind had numbed his brain.

John couldn't go home. The FBI would probably be waiting for him. Maybe they had already ransacked his house, looking for terrorist evidence. If he checked into a hotel, paid with a credit card, they could soon trace him. There was nowhere to go but back to Christina's, like it or not. Maybe the Universal Mind, if there was one, was helping him stay on track with his ultimate desire—to be a screenwriter, but it felt more like the universe was forcing him. He might as well jump in with both feet. Yes, even into bed with her. If he wanted her cooperation, he knew he would have to accept her the way she was, and like it. And maybe he did like the way she was. She was anything but boring.

A gardener's truck was parked in front of the house. John eyed it suspiciously, looking for human occupants, especially FBI types. The truck cab was empty.

He rang the bell a couple of times, but Christina didn't answer. He anxiously punched in the code and opened the door. "Christina!" Christina!" She didn't answer. *Maybe she's in the backyard, or maybe she was taken back to the sanitarium. Or maybe the FBI is questioning her.* He shook his head. *Naah. Don't think they know where I am.*

He walked to the kitchen, looking around all the while for intruders. Then he shook his head, hoping to clear his suspicions. "This is ridiculous," he said aloud. "Do I have spend the rest of my life looking over my shoulder?" He gave half a thought to contacting the FBI to get it over with, whatever it was going to be. *No. Better call Ross from a pay phone later, if I can find one these days, to find out what's going on.*

He saw her in the garden through the French doors, talking to a gardener and pointing to different areas of the yard. John stepped out onto the blue slate patio with thyme and purple and white alyssum growing in the cracks between the slabs. He smiled. The little patio seemed so like her. She turned and gave him a dazzling smile. As beautiful as ever. After a moment of finishing her conversation with the gardener, she approached him. The gardener seemed to be scowling as his eyes followed her to John. John glanced at the gardener. *I guess I'm not the only one captivated by her charm.* He smiled knowingly at the gardener, who only continued to scowl.

What's with him, John was wondering, only to forget all thought of the gardener as Christina touched his arm tenderly.

"I called your office, but they said you don't work there any more. Then they asked who I was and where you were."

"What did you tell them?" he asked gruffly.

"Nothing. I just said I was a friend and didn't know where you were. Then I hung up. What happened?"

He shook his head. "It's a long story. I'll tell you later. Do you have caller ID blocking on your phone? Do they know your number now and where you live?"

She thought a moment. "I don't remember." Her eyes searched his face softly. He couldn't take the tender way she was looking at him. He turned his eyes away.

"Let's go in," she said, taking charge and taking his arm. "I'll fix us some lunch."

John went with her in something of a daze. He didn't know what to do next. Eating seemed as good as anything. He opened cabinet doors until he found the dishes. He set out a couple of plates and glasses on the kitchen table. "Got any beer? Or wine?"

"No beer, but there's a bottle of chardonnay in the fridge, uh… I know it's not supposed to be chilled according to the experts, but I like it cold."

"So do I," he said as he took the wine out. "Where's a corkscrew?"

She pointed to a drawer. "I'm making a chef salad, sort of. With turkey and cheese, and we have some crackers somewhere. Will that be enough for you?"

"Sure. Sounds good. I gotta watch my youthful figure."

Christina laughed. She finished making the salad and put it on the table. She found some crackers. They no sooner sat down than the doorbell rang.

"Don't answer it, Christina. It's probably the FBI looking for me." The doorbell rang again. "This salad looks delicious," he said. "Pass me some of those crackers. I should tell you what happened. I did something stupid. Probably the stupidest mistake I ever made."

"Why would the FBI be here? Did you commit a crime?"

"No. Nothing criminal, just a stupid mistake. Uh... I don't know how to begin. Uh... I guess I'll start with, your story intrigued me. I wanted to write a screenplay, but I could never seem to get anywhere with my own ideas. I was going to tell you... ask you if I could uh..." He looked up at her. She was looking out the window, alarm on her face. He looked out. There were two men in dark suits staring back at them through the window of the kitchen door.

"Stay here." John pushed back his chair and stood up. He faced them through the closed door.

"Mr. Davis?" One of them said loudly through the glass. "We need to talk to you."

John opened the door just enough to step through to the outside. He closed the door behind him. "What is it?" he asked as if he didn't know.

The man on the left glanced back at the gardener, who was leaning on his hoe and watching them. "Can we go in? We want to speak to you in private."

Not one to stay out of things, Christina joined them outside.

"Christina. Go back in the house. This doesn't concern you."

"If it concerns you, it concerns me. What is this about, gentlemen?"

"That's what we want to know," someone said behind them. All four turned around. Two more men had seemed to appear out of nowhere.

"Who are you?" one of the dark-suited ones asked.

The new guys whipped out their cards.

"Oh, NSA poking your noses into FBI business again, eh?

"Well, Bob, like the lady says, if it concerns you, it concerns us."

"You two know each other?" Christina asked.

"Yeah," Bob the FBI man said. "Only too well. These guys are always following us around like we can't do our jobs without them."

"Just exactly what is your job here?" she asked rather impertinently.

Bob looked at the gardener. The gardener started hoeing some weeds to show he wasn't interested in their conversation. "Hey, you there! Why don't you a break and come back tomorrow!"

John said, "I like witnesses." To the gardener he said, "Stay. Go on with your work." John approached the gardener. Bob followed him. The gardener was avidly breaking up a brightly blooming bed of flowers with his hoe.

"Hey! What are you doing?" John grabbed hold of the hoe. The man held on. "Christina ask you to chop up her flowers?"

The gardener let go of the hoe and ran. Everyone took off after him, but he got to his truck and made his getaway before they could catch him.

"Was that one of yours?" Bob asked the NSA guys.

"Hell, no! Our guys know what to hoe and not to hoe. Who else is snooping around here?"

"CIA, maybe," Bob said. "They can be pretty stupid. Sure blew his cover."

"Yeah," the other men agreed.

"Look. We're not going to knock you off or beat you up, or even arrest you. We just want to talk. There might be other ears hiding in the bushes. Can we go inside now?"

John studied their faces. They didn't seem so threatening after his encounter with the flower killer, so he said okay.

Christina showed them into the living room. No one seemed to want to sit down at first.

"Please," she said, being the first to sit down. "Have a seat, then we'll talk." Reluctantly, one by one the men sat down, leaving John standing alone. "John, please." Christina entreated, patting the sofa cushion. He sat down next to her on the sofa.

Bob started the questioning that John had been dreading. "Ross told us what you claim happened. Now you wanna tell us in your own words why you wrote that ridiculous crap and put it in the paper?"

John looked at Christina. "I'm sorry. I didn't get a chance to explain it to you, Christina. I was going to tell you, really, and get your permission. It was an accident."

"Permission for what?" she asked.

Bob broke in. "I'm doing the questioning. Just keep quiet."

"Before I answer anything, who are you people?"

"Fair question. I'm Bob from the FBI. This is Steve from the FBI, and…" he motioned to the other two.

"I'm Jim, NSA."

"Oliver, NSA."

John stood up. "Oliver? Jim? Bob? You guys make these names up?" No one answered. "You got any ID?"

"Idee about what?" Bob quipped as he fished out his wallet. The guys chuckled.

John rolled his eyes. "As if everybody hasn't already heard that joke about Bush's traffic stop." He went around to each man and studied his ID.

Christina spoke up. "How do we know you're not aliens?"

"We're U.S. citizens, just like yourselves," Bob answered.

"Extraterrestrials. I've been watched by them for some time. Maybe for years."

"If anyone's an alien, it'd be that gardener you hired."

Jim laughed. "Yeah. The CIA'll hire anybody."

"I've been using the same gardening service for years, but he's not the regular guy. They must have hired a new one."

"Okay," John said, going back to his seat. "It went like this. I got a letter from Christina here, back in November…"

"How'd you meet her?" Oliver interjected.

"I didn't know her when I got the letter. She had some experiences which led her to believe that there was an extraterrestrial plot of some kind to take over Earth. She wasn't sure if it was true or if she was imagining it so she went to a psychiatrist. Instead of trying to get to the truth of the matter, he persuaded her to commit herself to an institution. All they did was medicate her. They didn't try to help her. Her friends abandoned her, she had no family, her parents had recently died in an auto accident. She had seen me on TV, thought I seemed nice enough, uh, compassionate enough that I might be willing to listen."

Bob interrupted him. "But how did it end up that you published her imaginings in the paper? That doesn't seem very compassionate."

"I became fascinated with her story, real or not. I'm a writer. I'd been thinking of writing a screenplay. Her story seemed like something I could get into. One excruciatingly boring day in the newsroom I got a flash of a scene for it, so I wrote it down." He turned to Christina. "I'm sorry. I was going to talk to you, get your permission. Your real identity would never be revealed. I thought maybe we could write it together."

"It's all right, John. Except the part where you published it in the paper before you talked to me. Why did you do that?"

"It wasn't intentional. I brought my laptop to your house because I had to finish the article that I was supposed to write for the morning paper. I finished writing the article, but before I sent it, I thought I would retrieve the scene I had written at work on the office computer. I opened it and left it on my desktop. Just as I was getting ready to send my article, Christina walked in. I got flustered because (a) I didn't want her to see the scene until I had a chance to get her permission, and (b)..." he smiled at Christina, "every time this beautiful woman walks into a room I get flustered. I spilled my coffee, copy and pasted what I thought was my article, addressed the e-mail, sent it, and shut off the computer before she could see anything. Unfortunately, I had sent the wrong thing, sent them my scene."

"Didn't someone at the paper notice what you sent? Don't they proof your copy? Approve it?"

"Not always. I've been there for years. They all know my grammar is impeccable and my articles press worthy. The formatters are always up against a deadline. They don't read anything. They're lucky to get the lines and pages in order by press time."

"Sounds lame enough to be true," Oliver said. He looked at Christina. "Let's see if there's evidence of spilled coffee. Christina, show us where it happened."

They all traipsed upstairs and followed John to his room. He showed them the spot which he hadn't cleaned very well.

Bob nodded his head. "Well, there's the spot, guys. What's the verdict?"

Oliver said, "Too clever a plan for terrorists. Maybe they just wanted publicity for their upcoming film." Nods of agreement from the others, except for John.

"I told you I only had hope she'd agree. There was no plan yet for a film, and I'm not conniving enough or stupid enough to have thought of losing my job for a little publicity for something not even written yet!"

"Maybe," Bob said as he walked out the door and started down the stairs. "But you can be sure we'll be watching for any more unusual publications from you."

"Fat chance you'll ever see any publication of mine again. I've been fired, if you'll recall. Not likely to be hired by anyone else, either." They all followed Bob down the stairs to the front door.

"Well, you could change your name, get a false ID, Social Security number, become someone else," Oliver joked with a self-satisfied smirk.

"You want to get one for me?" John asked him. "It would make my life a lot easier."

"Gee, I don't think I know how to do that. Sorry."

John opened the front door for them. The men left without another word, and with a sigh of relief John shut the door.

"Wow!" Christina responded. "I had no idea it was like that for you. Sorry if I distracted you at the wrong time."

He turned to her, put his hands on her arms, pulled her close. "There is never a wrong time." Then he kissed her, and she kissed back.

She said, "I was wondering when you'd get around to this." They kissed again, and then she said, "We should check out the carpet in your room—see if it needs more cleaning."

"I'm sure it does, but I'd rather do some more kissing up there instead of checking carpets," he said, caressing her hair.

She took his hand and led him up the stairs.

When they awoke in each other's arms in John's bed, the sun was setting. "Mmm," Christina murmured, snuggled up against John's chest. I haven't felt this safe in a long time."

"Don't let it fool you," John laughed. "I'm more after you than anyone is."

Christina laughed, too. "I like having you after me, but why would you be after a crazy girl like me?"

"I like your craziness. I'm in love with your mind. It's so free of convention, or constriction."

"This is the first time a man ever said he loved me for my mind. I like it. As for the screenplay, it's okay with me. I promised to pay you for looking out for me. So I could pay you more for working on it."

"I don't want your money. I have to find a job somewhere, then we can work on the screenplay."

Christina got up and was putting on her clothes. "Look, I have…"

"Yeah, I'm looking." He eyed her slender body up and down. "Looking at a beautiful woman I'm happy to have in my life."

"I have plenty of money, John, in the range of nine figures. You're not going to break me, and as far as I'm concerned, it will be money well earned by you."

I'll think about it later." He got up and started dressing. "Right now, I'm thinking about my empty stomach. We never finished lunch."

—⁓—

After dinner, John brought his laptop downstairs. Christina sat down on the sofa with him. He said, "I'm thinking maybe we should write a book first. I know people in publishing. I got free publicity from the paper already, and notoriety sells! If we act fast, we might find a publisher to work with us who could hook us up with Hollywood."

"Why not produce the film ourselves? I've got the money."

"I think it's better to go with professionals, an established company. Now some questions for you, my sweet. First, why all the books about aliens supposedly coming to earth… alien abductions and so on?"

"Some of them were my mom's. We shared an interest in that. I… um… never told her of my weird dreams, though, that I've had since I was about six. The other strange events, well they seemed to start happening after she died. After they died."

"Did she have any weird dreams that you know of?"

"She never mentioned any, but she did believe alien abduction stories are true. She said she thought she was abducted once when she was driving down to L.A. on the 5 to meet my dad who was down there on business. She had gotten a late start, so it was getting dark. Suddenly she saw a blinding light coming at her. That's all she remembered. Three hours later she awoke in her car by the side of the road, about ten miles south of where she had seen the light."

It must be hereditary. "Was your mom schizophrenic?"

Christina huffed audibly and got up from the couch. "You don't believe me, do you? What you're really asking is am I schizophrenic, and did I inherit it from my mother!"

"No, no," he protested. "I just wanted to rule it out. Plenty of otherwise normal people claim to have been abducted by aliens." Trying to smooth things over, he added, "I want to read some of your books. You pick out a couple you think are authentic and I'll read them. I know next to nothing about the phenomenon."

Somewhat appeased, Christina went into the library and searched the titles. She came back with two books and placed them on the coffee table.

"What's the first strange dream you remember having?"

Christina stared at him a moment, then said, "We'd been on a trip to New Mexico when I was six. All I remember is there was a small narrow stairway carved into the side of a cliff. I looked down there, but I didn't go down the steps. They were too scary. A couple of months later I dreamed I was to be a human sacrifice for a tribe of primitive people. My parents and my brother and sister were standing there with the natives. I thought we three children were all to be sacrificed. The natives made me go first. I thought that was strange because my sister was the oldest. She should go first. I really didn't know if the others were going to go at all. Maybe it was just me. I had to walk up the narrow stone steps like those in my dream. There was a bathroom sink at the top with faucets, if you can believe that, and I was supposed to put my head down in it and my head would go into the drain, and that would be it. It was just a little drain, like in any bathroom sink."

"Wait!" John interrupted. "You have a brother and a sister?"

Christina shook her head sadly. "Not any more. They died two years ago."

"I don't believe it! Everyone in your family died? How did they die?"

Christina sighed. "My sister fell off a balcony and my brother was walking across the street when he was killed by a hit-and-run driver."

John was astounded. "How could your sister fall off a balcony?"

"No one knew how or why."

"Was she depressed, maybe suicidal?"

Christina shrugged her shoulders. "She didn't seem to be."

"It's no wonder you had a meltdown when your parents died."

"Anyway, in the dream, I put my head down in the sink. All there was was blackness.

"I think all their deaths were some kind of conspiracy, by alien beings, or human beings who thought we knew something we weren't supposed to."

John couldn't pay attention any longer. His mind was racing and his heart was pounding. He had the unbelievable thought that she had done away with all of them so she would be the sole heir to millions. He had to get some distance from her and calm down, think things out clearly. He got up from the couch. "I really have to get out of here."

"You're right. We're not safe here. I'm going to get another place where they can't find us. Let's do it tomorrow."

"I meant I'm tired and need to get some sleep." He fumbled around in his mind for a way to tell her he wanted to be alone, but he couldn't come up with anything. He simply said, "I'll see you in the morning." He grabbed his laptop, yanked the plug from the wall. Christina stared at him silently as he headed up the stairs.

John couldn't sleep. It was a crazy idea that this beautiful, soft, tender woman could have killed four people. Well, she was crazy, wasn't she? Maybe the whole thing was an act to make people think she was innocent, so affected by the death of all her family that she had totally flipped. Did she really expect people—him—to believe that aliens killed them off? He had to get out of there. Disappear.

On the other hand, she didn't know what he was thinking. Surely she wouldn't kill him because she wanted his help in making a movie. But he no longer wanted to help her make the film. He wanted to go home.

Or maybe it was all just coincidence. Maybe she had nothing to do with their deaths, maybe she had been truly overwhelmed. As much as he wanted to run, he wanted to stay. He tossed and turned for hours, had short intervals of fitful sleep and nightmarish dreams. He got up at three in the morning, got dressed. It was chilly, so he put on his jacket. A good excuse. He really put it on because he was thinking he might just get in his car and drive away.

Little night lights cast a dim and eerie glow around him as he headed for the stairs, then down to the kitchen. Why did she hold onto this huge house, memories everywhere that must constantly remind her of her loss? Or was this what she killed for? He roughly shook his head to stop the thoughts as he turned on the kitchen light.

Christina was there, looking out the patio door. She spun around when the light came on. She was holding a gun, pointed at John. He froze when he saw it. They stared at each other for an eternity, their eyes wide with fear. *Move! Go!* His flight mechanism finally kicked in and he turned and ran from the doorway. He kept running, through the dining room, through the living room toward the front door. He grabbed the handle. It was locked. His hands shook as he fumbled with the lock.

"John!" she called from the other side of the living room. "Wait!" She waved the gun in the air as she came closer. "I didn't mean it!"

He finally got the door unlocked and put his hand on the handle to open it. She grabbed his arm and pulled.

"I wasn't going to shoot you! It was them!"

John turned and took hold of the gun with his free hand. She let go readily.

"What the hell were you doing? You could have killed me!"

"I heard voices in the yard. I saw aliens out there! When you turned on the light, I thought they were in the house! They want to kill me because I know what they're up to!"

John said nothing. He went back to the kitchen and looked out the patio door. He saw nothing but the dim outlines of a couple of trees in the fog. He switched on the floodlights. A few feet away a raccoon reared up on his hind legs and stared at them.

"Look," he demanded, pulling her to the door. "Is that your alien?"

She looked at the raccoon, then pulled away from him. "I don't expect you to believe me. No one does. But we're getting out of here. I'm gonna rent a house somewhere where they can't find me. Today!" She got the coffee beans out and poured some into the grinder. John waited to speak until the grinder stopped.

"You have any more guns in the house?"

"No. I had that one in the drawer by my bed."

The bullets plunked on the table and rolled as he emptied the gun. He gathered the bullets up and put them in his pocket. He sat down at the table and watched her warily as she put a plate of muffins in the microwave.

"I don't believe you, and I can't go on with this," he said.

She turned around. "What do you mean? You can't go on with what?"

"You. Your delusions. Your unpredictability." He was still holding the empty gun. Now he stuffed it in his jacket pocket.

She put a mug of coffee in front of him, and the plate of warmed muffins. John took up the mug. "I hope that's decaf at this hour." She nodded faintly and got herself a mug of coffee and sat down across from him. She took a sip of the coffee, then another. She set the mug down and stared into it, toying with it a little. "I'm sorry," she whispered.

The homey aroma of the warm muffins enticed him and he took one, carefully peeled the paper off and took a big bite.

Christina continued her examination of her mug. She understood how he felt, and thus could find no words to convince him to stay. Only the muffins seemed to hold him there. He took another one and repeated his ritual of paper peeling. She wanted to melt down into her chair to oblivion.

John finished the second muffin and washed it down with the coffee. He sighed heavily. They sat immersed in a silence that seemed unbreakable.

Finally, Christina got up and turned off the coffeepot. "I'm going back to bed," she said and walked out of the room. John sat there a while longer, trying to find the energy to leave, to even think about leaving, but he had none. He was drained, dead tired, his mind wouldn't function. It was all he could do to get out of the chair and climb the stairs to his room. He locked the door behind him and fell across the bed.

8

John opened his eyes. The sun was streaming in his window. He sat up with a start and looked out. It was late, he knew, because the heavy fog of the night before had burned off.

He found Christina downstairs in the kitchen, sitting at the table and talking on the phone. He poured himself a cup of coffee and grabbed one of those delicious muffins. He warmed it in the microwave for 25 seconds.

"The place sounds perfect," Christina was saying into the phone. "We'll see you then." She shut off the cell phone and set it on the table. John looked at the phone as he sat down.

"That's my phone you used. Where are we going?"

"I didn't think you'd mind if I used your phone. I'm afraid they listen in on mine. I don't want them to know where we're going."

"We? Where do you think I am going with you?"

"I think I've found a place to rent in the Russian River area. Please come with me to look at it. I'm really sorry about last night. It won't happen again."

John sighed heavily. He was still intrigued by her story. He still wanted make the film. *If only she would be just a little more normal, life would be a lot easier. But then there would be no story, would there?* "All right," he said as he got up from the table, "but after we look at it, I have to go by my apartment to get some clothes." He wanted to go after they went up north, not before, and he wanted to go alone. He didn't want her to know where he lived. He wanted an easy getaway if it became necessary, a place to be alone and think, without her interrupting, confusing his mind.

"Why don't you just move out of there? It seems like a waste of money to keep paying rent when you're not going to be there."

"Maybe later. Right now I need a place to write the script undisturbed."

"I won't do anything to disturb you while you're working."

He smiled. "You don't have to do anything. Your lovely presence in the same house can be very distracting."

"I'm afraid to be alone. I want you to stay with me."

They drove up the 101 in silence, except for occasional directions that Christina read from a map John had printed from the Internet. Their lighthearted closeness had been shattered by the gun incident. John didn't know if they would ever regain it. He felt he would have to be on guard from now on, watching for her to go off the deep end again.

Soon redwood trees were hovering over the road. He thought the road looked familiar. "Isn't this the road to Forest Vale?"

"I'm not sure. I didn't drive myself here, and you drove me out. You're not thinking of trying to take me back there, are you?"

"A sane man would do just that, but I don't seem to be one."

9

John was in the kitchen, drinking coffee and watching the rain pour down.

Christina came in looking confused. "John! Where are we? How did we get here? I don't remember!"

"What?"

She sat down at the table. "I remember calling about a house to rent... and I remember riding in the car with you... and I remember you mentioning Forest Vale." She shook her head. "That's all I remember."

John poured her a cup of coffee. "Here, maybe this'll help. It'll come back to you in a minute."

Christina took the cup and inhaled the warm, steamy aroma, took a sip. She put the cup down and ran her fingers through her hair as if trying to clear her mind. "How long have we been here?"

"Three days."

"Three days! I've lost three days?"

"Four, actually. We looked at this place four days ago and moved in the next day. Maybe when I asked if we were on the road to Forest Vale you got freaked out. You were wondering if I was taking you back there."

"What have we been doing all this time?"

"Well, we drove up here and looked at the house. When you saw the big round bathtub with the big window looking out onto the garden, you announced we'd take the place. We went back to Larkspur, you packed your bags, then we went to my place and I packed my bags. Then we went to your bank and got a pile of cash, most of which you made me deposit in my bank, which wasn't easy, because they suspected me of something, I don't know what, but eventually they let me deposit it. Then I wrote a check on my account for the deposit and the rent."

She looked at him warily. "Are you one of them?"

"What? One of who? No, Christina!" He stood up and came up behind her and put his hands on her shoulders. She shrugged his hands off. "You bought a piano the other day," he said, "and it was delivered yesterday. Look in your purse. You'll find the receipt, signed by you!" She found her purse, and the receipt. She stared at it, studying her signature carefully. Then she went into the living room and saw the ebony seven-foot Steinway grand sitting there.

"Why would I buy a piano? Whose idea was that? Is this part of the plan to confuse me?"

John took her hands and put his face close to hers. "It was entirely your idea. You bought it for me. I told you I played the piano, so you bought one."

"Prove it to me," she said. "Play something for me."

John went over to the piano and sat down. He rubbed his hands together. "I'm a little rusty. I might make mistakes."

"I don't care. Just show me you can play."

"What would you like to hear?"

"Stardust."

"I don't remember that one."

"I thought not." She turned abruptly and left the room.

John rolled his eyes and muttered, "Oh my God." Then he played "Night and Day." After that he played "Puttin' on the Ritz." Once he got into it, he forgot everything else, and played song after song. He stopped for a moment to think of something, and noticed Christina sitting on the sofa. He got up and went over to her. Tears were streaming down her face. He sat down next to her and put his arm around her.

"Sorry I doubted you. You play wonderfully. No wonder I bought a piano. I hate not being normal. Losing my memory. I think I'm losing my mind, too."

"It's okay. I'll help you remember. If it bothers you too much, we won't do the screenplay. We'll just forget about it."

"No, No! That has to be done. People have to know what's going to happen. Have I been here all the time? Maybe there was a while I was alone, and got abducted."

"Except for half an hour three days ago when I took a walk, you haven't been alone. Half an hour isn't enough time for anything to happen."

"Oh yes it is! How could you have left me alone in this secluded place, miles from anywhere!"

"You were the one who wanted to live in seclusion. Anyway, the CIA knows we're here. That should be some sort of comfort for you. They'll protect us from aliens."

"How do they know we're here? Did you tell them?"

"No. They just know everything. When I returned from my walk, I found my laptop propped up against the front door."

"So they snuck up here while you were gone. Anybody could have done that. Especially aliens."

He ignored her alien remark. "Have you had these memory lapses before?"

Christina got up from the couch. "I don't want to talk about it. Just leave me alone."

"Okay, Okay. I'll stop questioning you."

At that moment they heard the sound of a helicopter overhead. "What's that?"

"Just a helicopter, Christina. Let's go out and see."

"I don't want to go out," she said emphatically.

John went out by himself and looked up. It was a red helicopter. "It's a rescue copter," he called through the open door.

She ventured outside and stood next to John. "Where is it?"

"It already passed by." He put his arm around her shoulder. "Why don't we go in and have some breakfast? I'll fix you some pancakes."

Christina couldn't help smiling. "That's sounds good. I didn't know you could cook."

"A few things. Eggs, steak, pancakes, water."

"Water?"

"Yeah. I can boil water. You've heard of people who can't even boil water? Well, I'm not one of them." He kissed her on the tip of her nose as though she were a child. She giggled like one, and they went in.

After breakfast they cleaned up the kitchen. Then John positioned himself at the kitchen table with his laptop. "I'm going to work on our screenplay some more," he said. "I've been making good progress since we've been here."

"I think I'll get my laptop, too. I want to research some things on the Internet."

"We can't get wifi out here. Too many trees and hills. We've got cable DSL. You have to connect on my network."

"How do I do that?"

"Get your computer and I'll fix you up."

They spent a pleasant morning across from one another at their laptops, until Christina screamed. "They're in my computer! They've taken it over!"

John turned her computer to look at it. There were large icons of alien faces across the page. Christina slammed the lid down.

"It was nothing, Christina. You've got an older Mac. Sometimes when you convert a pdf file with images from the Internet to a text file, that happens. The images show up as icons of aliens. I've seen it before, really."

Christina pushed her chair got up from the table. "I don't believe you!" She ran into the bedroom and slammed the door.

John went after her. He tried turning the knob, but the door was locked. "Come on, Christina," he said through the closed door. "Open up. It's nothing, I swear."

"I want to be alone! Just leave me alone!"

"Okay. I'll be in the kitchen if you need me."

After about an hour, Christina came out of her room. She sat down at the table with John again.

"I removed all the alien pictures from your computer."

"I hope you didn't remove the notice about a meeting of people who've been abducted by them."

"Meeting? Oh, yeah, I saw that. No, I didn't remove it. Do you want to go?"

"If you'll go with me."

"Sure, but I'm surprised you'd want to go to something like that. It might upset you more. Have you ever been to one?"

"No. I want to find out what's happening, what other people have experienced."

"Don't you think it might make your sensitive imagination go into overdrive?"

"I'm not as crazy as you think."

"Tell me, do you think you have been abducted?"

"I don't know. They wipe out your memory of it. I've had a few missing hours of time, but never four days before."

"Those weren't exactly missing. I'm a witness that you were right here with me all that time, talking and eating and sleeping and making love."

Christina eyed him with suspicion, then changed the subject. "How's the screenplay going?"

"All right. I still have a long way to go, though."

"Crop circles. Did I mention how crop circles, especially the religious ones, are to make us think Jesus is returning?"

"Yeah, you mentioned it when we went out to dinner the other night."

"We went out to dinner? I went out at night?"

John had to laugh. "Yes, and you enjoyed it very much, after I got us a table twenty feet away from anyone else. I told you I thought crop circles were caused by the military. They started out simple, then, as they honed their laser weapons and skills, they drew more and more complicated patterns on the ground from an aircraft drone or a satellite, operating the equipment remotely. And sightings of the Virgin Mary, angels, and UFOs could be holograms projected by the military as well."

"Why would they want to make religious holograms?"

"Just practicing. Testing to see how people react. It might be useful in battle someday. Maybe they already use it in battle to confuse the enemy."

"You should use crop circles in the screenplay," she said, then did one of her frequent subject changes. "Something woke me up last night. A whirring noise. I looked out the patio door."

"Why didn't you wake me up, and for that matter, how can you remember that if you've forgotten everything else the last four days?"

"I don't know. Maybe my memory is slowly coming back. I just now remembered it. A craft of some kind was shining a light through the trees. I think they spotted me. They shined the light on me. It was blinding. I was paralyzed. I couldn't move. I don't know how long it was, or what happened after that. I think they erased my memory. The next thing I remember I was lying on the sofa. I got up and went back to bed. You were sleeping so soundly, I didn't want to wake you."

"Maybe it was a hologram."

"It was not a hologram!" she shouted.

"I really wish you'd consider taking your medication."

"I will not take any medication that will prevent me from getting the message to the world that an alien antichrist is coming. And since you don't believe me, don't expect me to talk to you any more… or sleep with you, either!" Christina walked briskly out of the room and into their bedroom. She slammed the door behind her and locked it.

John started to get up and follow her, but he thought better of it. This way he could work uninterrupted, at least until she decided to come out again.

Christina stayed in the bedroom for several hours, so John got a lot done on the screenplay, so much so that he was feeling burned out. He shut down his computer and picked up his cell phone. He hadn't checked his messages in days, not that he was expecting anyone to call after his denouement. Now was a good time, while Christina was in the other room.

He had several messages from Brad Scott. He called Brad. It would be good to hear a sane voice again, even if it was that of a crazy journalist.

"Hey, John. Where the hell you been?"

"Don't you know I got fired?"

"Yeah. Sorry to hear it, but it's the most interesting thing to happen around here. They didn't say you were fired, just that you left and wouldn't be back. I knew what that meant, especially after catching your last story. It was juicy. I want the details, man. Are you in love with her?"

There was a long silence before John answered. "I'd rather not be. It's more a writer's compulsion, I think. I gotta write her story."

"That bad, huh? Let's have lunch. I wanna hear the whole story."

"I'd like to get out of here for a while, pretend I'm sane. How about tomorrow, our usual hangout by the Ferry Building? I could use some sea air."

"Okay. You hiding out in Marin?"

"Worse than that."

"Where?"

"I'll tell you tomorrow."

Now all he had to do was convince Christina she'd be all right alone for a few hours. He knocked on her door. She didn't answer. He tried turning the handle, and the door was no longer locked, so he opened it and looked in. She was sitting on the unmade bed, leaning against the headboard, with a notebook in hand. "Hi," she said. "I'm making more notes for you."

He ventured over to the bed and sat down on it next to her. He propped up some pillows against the headboard, leaned back and put his feet up.

"Let's see." He leaned in close to her.

"They're not ready yet," she said putting the notebook aside.

"I'm sorry, Christina," he said, turning her face toward his gently with his hand and looking into her eyes. "I forget how sensitive you are." He kissed her softly.

"I'm sorry, too. Let's make up," she said, pulling the covers over them and kissing him some more.

It was only after they made love and had a leisurely dinner with ample wine that John expressed his desire to meet his friend and former business associate for lunch. She protested until he conjured up a story about how Brad knew people in the movie business. "All right, but I'm going with you."

John sighed heavily, trying to think of a response that would convince her it was better to meet with Brad alone. He wanted to get away from her for a while, get away from the stress of trying to keep her from reacting to every little thing. Get out of the creepy forest. See the sky, blue or cloudy, any kind of sky. See another face. Talk to another human being, a more sane one.

"I don't want Brad to get too intrigued with the mystery of you. He's a journalist, after all. You've got to stay here and let me handle it. It'll only be a couple of hours. Lock yourself in, turn on the burglar alarm. Keep your phone in your pocket in case of an emergency. You know there's really nothing to worry about."

"Yes, there is," she responded weakly.

"If anyone wanted to abduct you, they could have done it easily over the past year. No one has, because no one wants to."

She couldn't find an argument for that, so she reluctantly acquiesced.

———

The next morning Christina gave John a long, anxious kiss goodbye. He gave her reassurances that she could call him on his cell phone if she needed to, and that the alarm was activated, and maybe she should consider getting a big watchdog for the next time he might go to a meeting, promised to be home before dark, and so forth. The chilly, foggy mist enveloped him as he hurried to his car. He made a mental note to park his car in the garage next time.

The going was slow as he drove through thick fog out to 116 and south to just north of Petaluma to catch the 101. From there, the ground fog was lighter, and disappeared altogether by the time he arrived at the Larkspur Ferry. The sky was steel gray, the temperature forty-eight degrees according to his car thermometer, and when he parked the car and got out, he estimated the wind chill factor to be thirty–three degrees. He steeled himself against the wind as he walked to the ferry terminal. He had to wait only a few minutes before boarding.

Inside, he got a cup of strong, steaming coffee to warm his hands and insides with. He put a lid on it to keep it from spilling. The lounge was filling up with chattering passengers. He preferred the sound of the wind chilling his ears to the cacophony of loud conversations and cell phones ringing many different tunes at once.

Grasping his coffee cup, he stepped out onto the deck and positioned himself near the front of the ferry. Choppy whitecaps rocked the ferry, making it too much trouble to drink his coffee, but he clung to it for warmth, first with one hand, then the other, keeping his available hand firmly on the guardrail. He was the only fool out there in the cold, and his only thought was, "God, it's great to finally be alone with me as the only lunatic." He relished the stiff wind pelting his face with ocean spray for several minutes until his face was numb. When he'd had enough, he went back inside the lounge. By the time he found a seat, they were getting ready to dock.

Brad was waiting for him at a table in the restaurant. He jumped up and shook John's hand. "What the hell happened to you? You look like a drowned rat!"

John laughed as he took off his dripping parka and his wool knit cap. "It was great." His face was red with cold. They sat down. "I spent most of my time out on the deck. It's been so many years since I rode the ferry, I'd forgotten how invigorating it can be."

"You're crazy, Davis."

"Yeah," John grinned, "and lovin' it. You should try quittin' your job some time. It gives you a whole new perspective on life."

"Don't think I'm ready for that. Of course, the way things are now, it may be sooner than I think."

John picked up the menu. "Seems like years since I've been down here."

"It's only been a few days, John boy. Hey, tell me what's happening."

John shook his head. "Let me order first. I worked up an appetite this morning."

A brief inner battle ensued between his primal desire for a high fat, high cholesterol steak sandwich and his intellect calling for a sensible fish dish. The cave man won. John signaled the waiter, who took their orders and disappeared. "So what's new in the office? Who did Ross replace me with?"

Brad shook his head. "Nobody. He decided it was an opportunity to reduce the budget and see how high he can pile the work on us. I'm a little pissed at you for pulling that stunt and getting out of there."

"Hey, I did not do that on purpose. That woman had me so flustered I accidentally sent in a rough idea for a scene in a screenplay. Believe me, if I could take it back, I would. It wasn't even well written."

"Ain't that the truth! Looked like third-grade writing to me."

John's wounded ego raised his voice a little too much. "I said it was just a rough idea, a first draft!"

"Come on, I was only kidding. I know what a first attempt looks like. You gotta admit, though, it sounds a little lame. Who's gonna believe it could ever happen?"

"How many sci-fi movies are there that could really happen, Brad? What I want to know is do you know anyone even remotely connected in the film business?"

"I can't think of anyone offhand. I might know someone who knows someone, though. It'll take a little while to hunt around. Now that I have to work harder at the paper, I don't have much spare time."

"She'll pay you if you come up with something."

"Well, in that case, I'll take the job. Does she pay you for writing?"

"Yeah, I get paid, for writing, babysitting, uh… nursemaid. I get paid very well. Room and board, too."

"Is she as beautiful as her picture? Is she still in the mental hospital? Is she really crazy?"

"Yes, no, maybe."

"Are you…"

"Yes," John interjected, knowing what the question was going to be. He laughed. "What are you, a reporter?"

"It's in my blood. Can't help myself."

"Well, neither can I. I'm going to see this through. Just help me find someone to make her story into a film."

"I will if I can. This could be more interesting than my regular job, but what isn't?"

—∿∿—

After lunch, John stopped by his apartment to see if the CIA or other three-letter guys had trashed it and to pick up some clothes. The papers on his desk looked a little more disorderly than usual, but otherwise the place was the way he had left it—a mess of newspapers, books, assorted dirty clothes, etc. He gathered up his bills and laundry and headed back to the forest. He wondered briefly if he should give up his apartment, but it would be too much trouble to clear it out, and how much longer could he put up living with her anyway?

Christina was calmly watching television when he returned.

"You look calm for a change. What are you watching?"

She switched it off and got up. "It was a history program about Egypt. Something other than aliens to occupy my mind."

They embraced each other, kissed a little. "How did it go with your friend? Does he know anyone who can help?"

"He's not sure. He's going to look around. It might take a while. I was thinking, would you like to get a car for yourself, in case you want to go out and I'm not here?"

"But where would you be? I don't want you to go anywhere without me."

"I don't know. Just a thought."

"I don't ever want to drive a car again. Maybe somebody will tamper with it and I'll crash like my parents."

"How about a cruise? Would you like to go on one?"

"It sounds good, but if the aliens find me, I'll be trapped on a boat with nowhere to run." Seeming to want to hide at the mere thought of them, she buried herself in his arms.

He raised her face by the chin out from his chest. Well, then, how about a road trip? Tahoe, or we could drive up to Oregon. There are even more trees to hide in up there."

"Maybe," she murmured. "Casinos would be good, too. There's so much electrical energy there, it might foil their tracking devices for a while."

He smiled at her. "You like to gamble?"

"A little. Let's do it. But," she added, "let's go to Las Vegas! It'll be even more confusing for anyone trying to track me. Miles of slot machines."

"That's a lot farther. We'd have to go through the desert."

"It's still winter. It won't be hot. And it won't be snowing. And I've never been there."

"All right, you're on. How about tomorrow?"

"How about right now?" She wriggled free of his arms. I'll go pack. How long should we stay?"

"Does it matter?"

"I have to know how much to pack."

"Uh, four or five days? You can always buy more clothes if you run out, or have them cleaned."

"Buying would be more fun."

He was glad he got her to go somewhere. It seemed to energize her and put her in a happier mood. He only hoped it would last and that she wouldn't stay shut up in their room the whole time they were there.

John put their bags in the back while Christina carried her laptop into the passenger seat with her.

John got in behind the wheel and fastened his seat belt. "What are you going to do with that? You know if you go wifi they can track you," he said with a smile. He pushed the button on the garage door opener and started up the engine. "Put on your seat belt."

She did as she was told and strapped herself in. "So you believe me now that someone's tracking me?"

"Well, it could be the CIA. Really, no, I don't believe it, I just want you to give me your undivided attention and entertain me with your stories while we travel."

"I don't have any stories right now. I have to stop at my bank. We're going in that direction anyway."

"Okay. You planning another huge withdrawal?"

"I don't want to use credit cards. They might be able to track me that way, so I'm paying cash for the rooms, the gas, the food, the gambling. Actually, I'm going to give you the money to pay for everything so it won't look like you're a kept man."

"Aren't I one? Do I care?"

"You're not a kept man, you have a job, and you're on the job, on an expense account, so just have fun."

"Well, I can't have fun if you're messing around with your computer the whole trip."

"All right," she said and put the computer on the back seat. She gently rubbed the back of his neck and toyed with his hair.

"That's more like it," he said. I'm a little surprised you've never been to Vegas. How come?"

"I guess I preferred other vacations, like Hawaii, Tahoe, the south of France, Tuscany."

"Did you travel with your boyfriend?"

"Yes. We were together for three years. The last boyfriend, I mean. We were engaged when my parents died. He had difficulty putting up with my grief and the alien problem. I never saw him again after I was put into the sanitarium."

"Did you call him?"

"All I ever got was his voice mail. He didn't return my calls. That's true love for you. 'I'll love you forever, no matter what, except if you're crazy.'"

"Did you love him a lot? Were you devastated?"

"They had me on some strong drugs, so I didn't feel as upset as I might have otherwise. But also it wasn't that deep. I was nearing thirty and thought I'd better get married pretty soon if I wanted to have children. I loved him enough for that, I thought, and we had fun together. He was wealthy, too. It was hard to find someone who wasn't in love with my money more than with me. I certainly have proof now he wasn't after my money."

"What do you mean?"

"A money-hungry guy would have hung around, hoping I'd get better and marry him. Or marry me and get the court to appoint him conservator."

"Is that what you think about me? That I'm after your money? I'm not wealthy, but I'm not broke, either."

"No. I don't think you're after my money. You're after my story."

"Is that better?"

"I don't know yet. And I'm not sure about starting a family now. I don't feel stable enough. Maybe later on. There's still time. I want a normal life. I want children. I want a devoted husband who loves me for myself."

"You seem to be getting better."

"Maybe, but my thoughts about aliens have not changed."

"Maybe they don't have to. If your dream foretells the future, nothing is going to happen to you before Jesus lands. The pseudo-

Jesus, that is. Until then we can work on a way to warn people."

"That's my plan, John." She played with his hair some more. "I hope I can live more calmly. You've helped me a lot. I feel safer with you, and you manage to make me see some sense, anyway." She eyed him thoughtfully. "How you do feel about children?"

He smiled. "I like kids. I'm not the kind of guy, though, who'd rush into something like fatherhood, or who won't feel fulfilled if I don't have any. I've just been busy doing my job all these years. I haven't thought about it much." He took his eyes off the road to look at her. "Is this a prelude to a proposal?"

Christina laughed. "Not really. Just a fork in the road. My feelings for you are getting a little deeper. Wondered if I should call a halt to them."

"And?"

"I think I can let them go on for a while."

They stopped for a quick dinner off of I-5 about halfway to Bakersfield, then continued on to Bakersfield, where John filled up his gas tank. They decided to keep driving even though it was about nine o'clock. The highway was fairly empty, the weather was mild, and the starry sky was magnificent.

Christina stared anxiously out the window at the sky.

"I wish you could relax, Christina. There's nothing out there."

"Then what is that light in the sky following us?"

"I don't see anything. Probably just a satellite."

"Satellites travel east or west don't they? Not south. Something up there is following us. I don't like being out here alone in the middle of nowhere in the middle of the night. Let's go back."

John pulled over to the shoulder and stopped. He opened the door.

Christina grabbed his arm. "What are you doing? Don't go out there!"

John pulled his arm from her grasp. "I'm just going to take a look." He got out and moved to the front of the car as a semi roared by. He scanned the sky above. "There's no light up there except for stars!" he called back to Christina. Then he spotted an unusually large star above them. As he looked at it, it seemed to be growing larger. Now she's got me seeing things. He looked away and then looked at it again. It was definitely getting larger, getting closer, he thought. Stay calm, it's just your imagination. He returned to the car and for the briefest moment fumbled for the key before he turned on the ignition.

She saw through his attempt to appear calm. "You saw something! What is it?"

His foot hit the accelerator too hard and the tires squealed as they reentered the highway.

"Tell me!" she demanded, "What is it!"

"Nothing! It was nothing," he yelled. "My foot fell asleep. I couldn't control it."

"You're lying. I know you saw something." She rolled down the window and looked up. "There is it is! It's coming towards us! Faster, John! Faster! Get away from it!"

He rolled down his window and stuck his head out. The light was still above them, about the size of a full moon now. He sped up.

"Oh my God!" Christina shouted. "It's behind us!"

John looked in the rearview mirror. Yes, there were lights behind them. Bright lights. Red, blue, and white lights. "Shit!" He slowed down and pulled over.

The highway patrol officer approached on the passenger side and peered in the window at them. "Good evening, ma'm, sir. You were going eighty-five, sir. Let me see your license."

The officer pointed his flashlight into the car, looked them over while John searched through his wallet and handed his license over. The officer shined his flashlight on it, perused it. "Wait here." He went back to his patrol car and handed it to his partner.

Meanwhile, Christina was watching them in her side mirror. Then she gave John a sidelong glance. "Maybe they're, uh, aliens in disguise?"

John rubbed his eyes and face roughly. "Christina! Get a grip! They're giving me a big fat ticket for speeding! Thanks to your paranoia!"

The officer returned with a ticket book in his hand. "Where you headed in such a hurry?"

Christina answered. "We're going to Las Vegas."

"Oh. That explains it. In a hurry to lose your money." He walked around to the driver's side. "Have you been drinking?"

"No. I don't drink and drive."

The officer leaned down close to John's face and sniffed the air. "Okay. I'm not going to test you at this time." He wrote out the ticket. "Save some of your money for us." He held the ticket out toward John who took it reluctantly.

John turned on the overhead light and looked at the ticket. "Reckless driving and speeding! Come on. I wasn't being reckless."

"Eighty-five in the dark is reckless. A lot of wild animals out here. Hitting a coyote could kill you. Take it easy, now. Vegas will still be waiting to take your money tomorrow. We'll be keeping an eye on you."

"Thank you, officer, for looking after us," Christina said with the utmost sincerity.

The officer looked surprised. "Was his driving scaring you?"

Christina shook her head. "No, no. I just mean I'm a little scared at being out here on the lonely road late at night. I'm glad you're out here patrolling."

"Okay, ma'm. Now lighten up your foot, Mr. Davis, or you won't have to pay for a hotel room tonight, if you know what I mean." The officer stepped back and John started up the car.

Once they were on the road again, John said, "Christina, just don't tell me about any moving objects in the sky again. Keep it to yourself."

'All right, but you have to admit you saw it, too."

"The power of suggestion made me think I saw something. Maybe I just saw the moon."

"The moon's not out tonight."

John said nothing. Clenched his jaw and drove on. He looked in his rearview mirror. The patrol car was back there, following him at a distance. He felt somewhat comforted by that fact. He knew Christina was right about the moon—the moon wasn't out.

They checked into the Bellagio, a hotel decorated in an ornate Italian style. It was one of the most expensive hotels in Vegas. Christina had pointed it out from the street when she saw the immense fountain with dancing lights and cascading jets of water. She ordered a suite. Although they had cash and paid for two nights in advance, the hotel required a credit card on record. John had to use his, of course. Then they followed the bellman and luggage to the elevator. The bellman led them to their suite and opened the door. In the bedroom he unloaded the luggage, got a tip from John and left.

Finally, John broke the silence between them. "A luxurious place, Christina. You know how to pick them."

She smiled. "I'm pleased with it, even though it's one of the smaller suites. I didn't want to use all our cash at once. We can have some fun here. Can we go downstairs for a while?"

"I'm exhausted. Tomorrow will be soon enough."

He shed his clothes and crawled into bed. By the time Christina brushed her teeth and joined him, he was fast asleep.

John awoke to the aroma of strong hot coffee. Christina was sitting on the edge of the bed next to him, holding a cup for him. John sat up and took the cup and drank.

"No good morning?" she asked. "No kiss?" She puckered up her lips toward his.

John had to laugh. "You look like a fish with lipstick. Guess I'll have to kiss you, or your lips'll freeze up and you'll look like that the rest of your life." He gave her a brief but affectionate kiss.

"You seem a little grumpy. Didn't you sleep well?"

"I slept great. Straight through all the nightmares of aliens chasing us across the desert—and catching us. Your paranoia's contagious."

"I ordered breakfast. Bacon and eggs, whole wheat toast, and country fried potatoes. And a fruit bowl. Would you like your breakfast in bed?"

"You're changing the subject."

"I don't want to talk about aliens. I'm trying to forget about them and have a little fun."

John got up and pulled on clean undershorts, a pair of khaki shorts, and a t-shirt which Christina had laid out for him on a chair. Then they headed for the sitting room where breakfast awaited them under shiny silver-plated domes on a white damask covered table set for two with matching napkins and silver-plated flatware. He sat down and lifted his dome. He inhaled the aroma of the thick applewood smoked bacon.

"This is definitely worth the nightmares." Christina smiled and sat down across from him. He devoured about half his breakfast before he spoke again. "How about a swim after breakfast?"

"Maybe later. I forgot to bring a swimsuit. I'll have to buy one. I want to check out the shops here anyway. It's been forever since I went shopping. And I want to get my hair cut. And go to the spa. What do you want to do?"

"Go for a swim, see a topless show."

"I should have guessed. The clues were there. Man—Vegas—breasts. I think I would be embarrassed, all those breasts bouncing around."

"I don't think they bounce much. The show girls usually have smallish breasts so they won't bounce around. There'll be other women in the audience."

"How do you know that?"

John smiled sheepishly, "It wouldn't be the first time I've been to a Vegas show."

"Then I won't be depriving you if we go to the Cirque du Soleil instead."

What could he say—nothing.

They finished breakfast and went down to the lobby. Christina pulled out her map of Bellagio and located the hair salon. "I want to get my hair trimmed first." She handed him the map. "Which way do we go?"

"This way," he said, taking her hand. "Don't let them cut very much off. I love your long hair. I might as well get a trim, too."

"Maybe I should get it cut short and change the color so no one will recognize me."

"Don't you dare, Christina! Can't they track you anyway with their advanced technology? Your electromagnetic footprint or something like that. You could get bigger shoes, change your footprint," he teased.

Christina laughed. "Here's the salon. Let's see if they can take us now." They could, and did. Christina and John were installed in chairs next to each other.

"Don't take off too much of her hair. Just a little trim. And don't change the color." Christina's female hairdresser smiled and looked at Christina. "One of those controlling guys," she said.

"Yeah. Just ignore him. Take off about an inch."

"Okay."

So, they got their hair trimmed to each other's satisfaction, and made an appointment for poolside cabana massages for later in the afternoon. Then to the shops. First, Dior. John was offered a comfy chair to view and critique Christina's selections as she modeled them for him. "I'd rather just go out and walk around and come back when you're finished."

"No way. This is part of your job, ha, ha."

He sat there reluctantly, complimenting her on each outfit she chose, mostly casual clothes, and a gorgeous, soft and revealing white nightgown. When it came time to present the bill, she brought the bill over to him. She wanted him to pay with his credit card. "Why?"

"You know, tracking me," she pleaded sotto voce.

A little too loudly, he blurted out, "They can't do that with cards!" He looked at the 4-digit bill. "I don't have that kind of limit! Put it on your own card."

The clerk heard the raised voice and approached them quickly. "Is there a problem with the bill?"

"No," Christina said. She dug out her credit card and handed it to the clerk. "Have my purchases sent up to my suite, please."

Then they headed for Chanel. "John, please don't make a scene like that in a shop again. I was very embarrassed."

"You were embarrassed? I was embarrassed that I had to say no."

"Then why did you?"

"If I hadn't, I would have been even more embarrassed if they tried to run my card through and have the charge rejected."

"Well, I hope you're right that the aliens can't track where I am by my credit card purchases."

John sighed heavily, but said no more about it. They went into Chanel's. "Haven't you bought enough already?" What he was thinking was did he have to sit through another try-on session when he would rather be doing almost anything else. He hated shopping.

"I'm looking for something special to wear tonight. I want to dress up for a change. After this we're going to Armani's to get you something decent to wear. You could call the restaurant and make a reservation for dinner."

"What restaurant?"

"I don't care, as long as it's good."

"Steak?"

"That would be the Prime Steakhouse."

"Great. I'll step outside and call."

"Don't wander off."

"I'll be right outside the door."

Eagerly, John stepped outside. He called information, then the restaurant and made a reservation for seven. He loathed the thought of going back in the shop and waiting idly. He saw Armani's across the way, and wandered over to look in the window. Just how decent did she want him to look?

"Sir! Sir!" a woman called to him. He turned around.

"Yeah?"

"You're wanted inside."

He nodded his head and went back into Chanel's. The sales woman had disappeared and Christina was nowhere to be seen. Wearied of this shopping excursion, he sat down and idly thumbed through a *Vogue* for want of better reading material. *The vanities of the idle rich,* he thought. He put the magazine down. Maybe part of her problem was she had so much money she wasn't motivated to do anything worthwhile. *An idle mind is the devil's workshop.* He laughed quietly to himself at the thought of that old adage. Maybe there was something to that. She should have some worthy cause to fight for. Well, maybe her desire to get this film made was a worthy cause. He wasn't sure. Maybe people needed to wake up to the seduction of the media, the constant entertainment that was already provided without the help of extraterrestrials. He closed his eyes, leaned his head back in the chair.

She was shaking his shoulder. "John, you're snoring! Wake up. I'm finished here."

"I wasn't snoring. I wasn't even asleep."

"You were, too. Even the sales clerk heard you."

"She did not."

"I'll go get her. She'll tell you,"

"Please don't. Can we quit shopping and go play a few dollars in the slot machines?"

"Not yet, John. First I have to get you something to wear tonight."

"Armani?"

"Armani's good."

"Well, let's make it quick. Just to let you know, I'm not going to wear a tuxedo."

Christina smiled and shook her head. "I didn't expect you would. I'd suggest a black suit, though. You would look very impressive in it."

With the aid of a salesman they selected a summer-weight black suit with a huge price tag, a couple of shirts, silk ties, socks and shoes. John had the suit fitted, to be sent to their room when finished. "I'd better get some matching underwear," John quipped.

Christina started looking at the underwear. John pulled her away. "I was kidding. You can own my outer appearance, but my underwear is my own."

She laughed. "Okay. You wanna go gamble now?"

"Not yet. I'm hungry. Let's get something in that cafe over there."

"I'm hungry, too." They had sandwiches and sparkling mineral water, and split a piece of chocolate cake.

"Now," John said after paying the bill, "which way is the casino?"

The casino area was bathed in golden light. Italian splendor bordered on ostentatious. On the audio level, it was fairly quiet.

"It's pretty empty," Christina remarked. "Maybe it's not a good place to gamble."

"Early in the day, my sweet, and middle of the week. Maybe what you mean is it's not a good place to hide out. No crowd to get lost in." She darted her eyes his way. He could see a little anger and a little fear in them. "You wanna go somewhere else? Some place more populated?"

Christina scanned the casino. "No. It's okay. At least this way I can see them coming."

"And how would you know they're aliens?"

"Could we just stop talking about them? I said before, I want to get my mind off them and possibly have a good time for a change."

"Okay, okay." They arrived at some dollar slot machines. Christina stopped in front of one.

"This feels like a winner," she said. "Hand over some money."

"How much?"

"A hundred."

He fished a hundred-dollar bill out of his overstuffed wallet and handed it to her, then he kissed her. "For good luck."

"You play, too."

He fished out another hundred for himself.

Christina looked down the aisle of machines. "That one, two machines down, feels like a winner, too. You can play that one."

"Is that an order, to play where you tell me?"

"Of course not. But I'm psychic, and if you play the machine I tell you, you'll win."

"Okay, Madame Christina. Your wish is my command." He kissed her briefly again. He went over to the machine and started playing. He came back to her in about five minutes. "I see you're playing your last dollars. Mine are gone, too. Some psychic you are," he said kissing her on the cheek.

Christina shook her head. "These are the worst machines. Let's go somewhere else."

"It's probably the same everywhere. Casinos exist to take your money. The best odds are the crap tables and blackjack, I think."

"I want to see the Luxor, and Excalibur. And I want to take a gondola ride at the Venetian."

"We should get a map."

Christina pulled out a brochure from her purse. "There was one in the room." She handed it to John, who opened it up.

"Excalibur is pretty close," he said. "Let's walk over there. We might want to take a taxi to the other places. Two or three miles away."

"What time is it?"

John looked at his watch. "It's two-ten. Don't you have a watch?"

"I have a lot of watches, but I never wear them. I don't think we have time to go anywhere else. We want to go swimming and have our massages. Let's try a few more machines here and then go swimming. We can go sightseeing tomorrow."

John got out his wallet again. They sat next to each other at a couple of machines and put their money in.

Christina asked him, "Why isn't a handsome man like you married already?"

"Didn't you ask me this before?"

"If I did, I didn't get a definitive answer."

"Definitive answer, yeah. Like I have a definitive life. I lived with someone for a couple of years, but it didn't work out."

"Why not?"

"Who knows. Mismatched, not deep? Whatever deep is. According to her I was more in love with my job than with her."

"Oh, so she broke up with you."

"Yeah, but I was more relieved than sorry. It was too hard to pretend I was interested in the possibility of spending my life with her."

"Do you think there might be someone you'd want to spend the rest of your life with?"

"I think it's possible there might be someone I'd like to try to spend the rest of my life with. I wouldn't know the actual outcome until either we split up or died."

Bells started ringing on John's machine. They kept ringing.

"What did you win?" Christina leaned over close to him to look at his machine.

John was smiling a big smile. "I'm not sure, the numbers just keep getting bigger." Finally, the machine stopped making noise. "Looks like three thousand dollars. Not bad. It was your money. Do you want half of it?"

Christina laughed. "It's yours. Put it in your retirement fund."

"Are you going to let me retire?"

"Definitely not."

"I think I should retire from this machine, since it paid out."

"Why don't you try it just a few more times? Sometimes it's a prelude to the really big jackpot."

"Oh, sure," he said, not believing it for a minute. "All right. I'll play five more times, and then that's it. I'm not going to let it suck back my winnings." He played five times and nothing happened. He got up from the machine. "Just one last try," he said, and pushed the button one more tine. Again the bells sounded.

"See, John?"

The machine stopped at one thousand dollars. "Okay," John said, pushing the cash-out button. "I'm going to stop while I'm ahead."

Christina moved over to his machine. "I think it's going to pay more, so I'll try it myself." She put in a hundred, and played a few times, but got nothing but a few cherries and little payout.1 "I guess you're right."

"This was a fluke. They pay a small jackpot and you think they're going to keep on paying. I'd just as soon make this the last machine I play on this trip, and put it in my savings account. Let's go swimming now."

After John collected his winnings, they changed into their swimsuits and went down to the pool.

"This is gorgeous!" Christina said as they entered the pool area. "It looks like an Italian villa. I want a pool like this."

"I'd rather have one less crowded," John remarked as he plopped his towel on a chair and took off his pool shoes. He dove into the deep end and Christina followed. They swam a couple of laps, then he turned and grabbed her, held her close. "You're not thinking of moving again, are you?"

"Well, yes. I'm thinking of selling my house and buying something that has a pool area like this."

"Surely not in Vegas! It's a hundred and ten in the summer."

"No, not in Vegas. We'll look around when we get home, find something in Sonoma County. In the wine country. Maybe a vineyard."

"When are we going to have time to work on the screenplay, if we're running around looking at houses?"

"John! Look!" She pointed to a man standing near them by the pool.

"What? Just a guy."

"He's staring at me. Oh my God! He doesn't have a navel!"

John shrugged his shoulders. "Maybe he had plastic surgery to remove it."

"Why would he do that? No, he's an alien. They fixed him up to look like a human, but they forgot the navel. Why else would he be staring at me?"

"I don't know, maybe because you were pointing at him." John nodded at the man and smiled.

Christina lowered her voice. "Why are you smiling at him?"

"Just trying to make up for your pointing and staring."

The man squatted down at the edge of the pool, close to them. "Do I know you?" he asked John.

"Nah. My girlfriend here thinks you look buff."

The man smiled. "Thanks, sweetheart," he said to Christina. "You look pretty swell yourself."

Christina smiled nervously and moved slowly away. John followed her. "See, John? He can't even speak contemporary English."

"What do you mean? He sounded okay to me."

"'You look pretty swell.' From the forties or fifties. I've heard it in old movies. No one says that nowadays."

He took her hands and held them between his, close to his chest, kissed her briefly. "Your imagination is getting carried away again. Please try to control it, or we're not going to have any fun."

"I want to go home now."

"Now," John said, pulling her toward the pool steps, "now we are going to have our massages, then go upstairs and take a nap."

"All right," she acquiesced, "but after that we're leaving."

"Do you want to drive through the desert in the dark again?"

Christina rolled her eyes. "Okay, okay, we'll leave early in the morning."

"I think I saw a hint of a navel on him. Maybe it got filled with suntan oil or something."

"Sure, John, whatever you say." She followed John up the steps and out of the pool. A masseuse and a masseur were waiting for them in the cabana.

At 7:30 they were enjoying their filet mignon when Christina said in a hushed tone, "That man just came in." She nodded her head toward the entrance.

"What man?' John turned his head to look. "Oh, him. I suppose he wants to eat like the rest of us humans."

"He's following us."

"You. He'd be following you, not me, but he isn't following anybody. He just wants a good steak."

The maitre d' led the man in their direction. The man smiled and stopped at their table. "We meet again. He looked at Christina. "It must be destiny."

"Hi, there," John said. He put down his knife and fork. Christina stared at her plate and pushed her food around nervously.

"You look ravishing tonight, sweetheart. What are your plans for this evening?"

John replied a little gruffly, "We're planning on finishing our dinner."

"Sorry. I didn't mean to intrude upon a romantic evening. I hope you enjoy your meal."

"Thank you. Enjoy yours, too. The food is excellent here." John took up his knife and fork again and cut off a piece of steak.

"Good evening, then." The man continued on, following the *maitre d'* to a table. The man sat facing them.

"Whatever you do, don't leave me alone for a minute tonight."

John took her hand. "You don't need to worry. I won't. But believe me, he's just a guy, and quite possibly just attracted to you, you look so stunning in your new evening dress and your diamond necklace."

"I want to go back to our rooms. I'm afraid of him. I don't like the way he stares at me."

"Relax. Let's finish our dinner before we decide what to do next."

"Let's fly home tonight," she whispered.

John almost choked on his mouthful of steak. "I can't leave my car here! I have to drive it back. If you want to fly back to Santa Rosa, I'll take you to the airport."

"No! I can't be left alone."

John shook his head. "Then, unfortunately, you'll have to ride back with me."

"Leave your car. I'll buy you another, any kind you want."

"No," he said firmly. The waiter came over to take their dessert order.

"I don't want any," Christina said.

John ignored her. "We'll have two vanilla ice creams, and coffee."

"Yes, sir."

"I said I don't want any, John."

The waiter looked askance at John. "She wants it, she just doesn't know it yet. Two ice creams and two coffees. Decaf."

"Cream and sugar?"

"Do you want cream and sugar, Christina?"

"Yes. And make it chocolate ice cream for me."

Christina kept her head down close to the dish as she hurriedly ate her ice cream and drank her coffee clumsily with her head still down. Frequently she peered at the man out of the corner of her eye. He was eating his steak, occasionally glancing over at their table.

"Can we go now?"

John was still savoring his ice cream. "When I'm finished."

"Hurry up, please. I have to go to the bathroom."

John finished his ice cream quickly and downed his coffee. Then he signaled the waiter for the bill. He counted out cash and put it in the waiter's folder. John noticed the man motion to the waiter and take out his wallet. He also noticed the man hadn't finished his dinner. Although he knew Christina was more than ready to leave, he wanted to distract her so she wouldn't see the man getting ready to leave when they did, so he asked her, "Are you ready, Christina?"

"You know damn well I am!" She bolted up and headed at a fast pace for the entrance. John followed behind her and glanced back to see the man looking at them and getting up from his table.

They found the bathroom. "I can't go in there and hold your hand, but I'll wait right outside the door and won't let any men go in."

"I don't want to go in there."

"You said you had to go."

"Let's go upstairs. I'll use our bathroom."

John sighed heavily "All right, but we're coming back down and have some fun at the tables, okay?"

"I don't want to."

"Then you can stay in the suite and I'll come down by myself."

"No. Stay with me."

"Try to make me."

They walked on to the elevators. Another couple was waiting for an elevator. John discreetly looked around for the man from the restaurant. John saw him coming towards them. Now he was getting concerned. Maybe he was CIA or something. But why the strange speech Christina had referred to earlier? Maybe he watched too many old movies? An elevator door opened. A few people got off. John and Christina got on the elevator with the other couple. John quickly pushed the button to close the doors, but as the doors were closing, the man stuck his hand in to stop them and entered the elevator.

"We meet again," the man said. Christina tried to shrink into oblivion behind John. Neither of them acknowledged him. John waited for him to push his floor button, but the man just stood there staring at him.

"What floor?" John asked him.

The man looked at the bank of buttons. "Uh, top floor."

John pushed the top floor button, then pushed another button which was one floor lower than the other couple's—not his floor. He wasn't taking any chances.

"Y'all doin' some gamblin' tonight?"

He had changed his manner of speech! John was certain he did not have that drawl earlier.

The elevator stopped and John and Christina got out, John hanging back a little so Christina could go out first. Out of the corner of his eye as he stepped out, he saw the man's hand reach toward the button panel.

The doors closed.

"That man is definitely following us," Christina said. "Now what?"

"Now we take the stairs," John answered.

"But it's six flights up."

"Don't you want some exercise?" he teased.

"Not that kind, and not at this time of night. Not in high heels."

"Then we'll go down a couple of flights, catch another elevator."

They hurried through the stairway door and made it down one floor before they heard a door slam two or three flights above.

"This way," John whispered, opening the stairway door. They ran to the elevator and Christina pushed the elevator button. They waited anxiously. Finally, one arrived and the doors opened. The stairway door opened at the same time. John pushed Christina into the elevator and plunged in after her. He pressed the button as hard as he could to close the doors. The four other people in the elevator were startled by their actions. A hand reached in between the closing doors and they opened to reveal the man they were trying to avoid.

"Fancy meeting you here, Christina," he said.

"He knows my name. How do you know my name? Who are you? Why don't you have a navel?"

John continued the questioning. "What are you? CIA, NSA? FBI?"

"Yeah," the man said.

"Leave us alone," Christina said. "I know who you are. We both know who you really are. I've written it all down and sent it to… uh… Oliver at the CIA!"

The man laughed heartily. "You could send it to everyone in the country, and guess what? No one would believe you. They'd think you're both insane."

The elevator stopped and the two couples got off. "Call Security!" John yelled after them. His presence of mind had finally returned, and he pushed the alarm button on the elevator and then pushed Christina out the door and followed her out. Christina started running down the hall. John tried to catch up with her. He didn't want her to get cornered at the end of the hall. How could she run so fast in those high heels? He felt heavy, his legs seemed too short, couldn't seem to make them move fast enough. The man was close behind him.

At the end of the hallway, Christina came to a stop and spun around. She and John were cornered. The man joined them there.

"Now…" the man began. Christina reached into her purse and pulled out a gun, a little derringer.

"Now," she said.

John looked at her gun in amazement. "I thought you said you got rid of them all."

"Don't be fooled," she warned the man. "This little gun can kill you."

The man put his hands up. "Now look. I just wanted a chance to get more details about your experiences. The Home Office isn't satisfied with their reports."

"Well, they can see the movie then. It'll all be in there." At this point a security force arrived—a hotel security guard and two Nevada State Police officers. Their guns were drawn and pointed at Christina.

"Drop your gun and step back."

She didn't drop it. "You don't understand. This man is…"

"Drop it now!"

Reluctantly, she did as she was ordered.

"Now everyone step way back." The State officer moved forward and scooped up the derringer. "Anyone else got guns?"

John shook his head. The man said, "Yes, I've got one. I'm with Homeland Security." He started to reach into his jacket.

"Hold it!" the officer snapped. Put your hands up. I'll get it." He reached into the man's jacket and pulled a revolver out of a holster. "Okay, now slowly get out your ID." The man did as he was told. He took out his wallet and thumbed through several cards. Then he pulled one out and handed it to the officer. The officer scrutinized it. "How do I know this isn't fake?"

"You could call them, I guess, but they don't acknowledge undercover agents."

The officer shifted his gaze to Christina. "Why did you have a gun on this guy?"

"He never said who he was. He's not with Homeland Security. He's an…" Here she got a nudge from John's elbow. "He's been harassing and chasing us since dinner, and rudely staring at me in the pool earlier."

The officer gave Christina a once over look. "Well, I can see why he'd stare at you, especially if you were in a bikini."

"It wasn't normal. He's not normal. He doesn't have a…" Another nudge from John. "He doesn't have any reason to be chasing us." She leaned forward closer to the officer. "Maybe he's a rapist. You should check out his record."

John smiled slightly. Crazy or not, she could think on her feet.

"Let me see your ID, ma'm. Yours, too, sir," he said to John. They handed them over to the officer. "Do you have a permit to carry a concealed weapon, ma'm?"

"Yes. Do you want to see it?"

"Later. Why were you pointing a gun at Mister Roberts?"

"He was following us. He talked to us at dinner, then followed us into the elevator. He asked for the top floor. We got off the elevator early to avoid him, took the stairs for a flight, heard a stairway door slam above us, so we came out on this floor and got another elevator. Just as the door was closing, this man appeared again. He stuck his hand into the closing doors and stopped them and got into the elevator with us. John and I ran out and down the hall. He ran after us. I'm a wealthy woman, officer. I thought he wanted to rob me."

"The three of you have some explaining to do. You'll have to come down to the station with me." He called for backup to bring a car to the Bellagio.

They all went downstairs willingly and waited with the officer and the security guards for the car at the hotel entrance. When the car pulled up, the officer and the guards were distracted for an instant, and that was when the Homeland Security man, if that was who he was, bolted back into the building and disappeared into the casino crowd.

The officer in the patrol car got out. The first officer told him to go after the man. Then he told John and Christina to get in the back seat. "Maybe that guy isn't who he said he was. I'll check him out."

At the station they gave their statements detailing the events involving the alleged Homeland Security man. The officer decided that since the man ran away, he wasn't all he said he was and perhaps Christina was right about criminal intentions. They were allowed to leave after giving their Bellagio room number, how long they were staying, and their home address and phone number.

They got into a cab. John told the cab driver, "Drive around a few minutes, until we decide where we're going." To Christina he said, "That was a *swell* evening."

"Very funny," she replied sarcastically.

"It's not too late to do some gambling."

"I don't want to. He's still there. I want to go home."

John ignored the "home" part. He put his arm around her and spoke softly into her ear. "Keep your voice down. We'll go somewhere else for tonight—the Venetian, the Luxor. He won't find us again."

"How do you know that?"

"Intuition."

"I am so sick of this whole thing. Why am I being tormented by aliens, or humans, as you think, following me everywhere?"

"Look, Christina. I agree with you. That guy was weird. He tells them he's with Homeland Security and then he disappears. He put on a phony accent, and he knew your name. I think the government wants to find out what we're up to. They may think we're some kind of security risk."

"But why?"

"I guess because of what I wrote in the paper. And they know it has to do with you."

"If we go back to the Bellagio to get our stuff, that man could be watching for us, and follow us everywhere we go. Maybe he wants to kill us."

"I'll call the Bellagio and have them send our stuff over to our new hotel. If they want to charge us for their trouble, I'll put it on my card over the phone."

"Okay, but use the hotel phone, not your cell phone. Maybe that's how he knew where we were, when you called for a dinner reservation."

He leaned forward and touched the driver's shoulder. "We want to go to the Venetian Hotel now."

They got a suite and John called the Bellagio. The staff had already packed up their stuff because John and Christina were now a "security risk." They would send their luggage over with his car. Christina refused to stay out and gamble, so they went straight up to their suite.

Early in the morning they had breakfast in the suite, and then checked out, both watching their backs the whole time.

Watching his rearview mirror, John pulled off the freeway.

"Why are you getting off here?"

"I wanna see if someone's following us."

"Are they?"

"Don't seem to be."

He stopped the car and waited for a couple of minutes. No one else got off the freeway, so he got back on. "I hope you aren't too upset, Christina. You have to figure the guy doesn't know where you live or he would have shown up before. Didn't you say you had some kind of mandala planted in your brain to protect you from the aliens?"

"I never said it was to protect me. I wasn't sure what it was for. I thought maybe it was to preserve important memories to remind me I have a mission to complete."

"Well, maybe it also protects you from them being able to track you, to know exactly where you are. Obviously they haven't found you all these years. Could that be the reason?"

"Hmm. It's possible, I guess, but they did find me in Vegas."

"We don't know if Mister 'Swell' was one of them, do we? Maybe they figured out who I am, and my vehicle, and followed me to get to you. Or maybe he's one of the three-letter guys."

Christina shrugged. After that, she relaxed a little. His plan seemed to work. He still didn't believe aliens were after her but had applied some logic according to her beliefs to persuade her that they couldn't find her so easily.

The drive home started out uneventfully. Then Christina wanted to make space ships out of lenticular clouds. "Look! Two spaceships!"

"Where?"

"There," she pointed. Don't you see them?"

"I see a couple of lenticular clouds. They're shaped a little like UFOs, but believe me, they're not. They form before a storm. Looks like there'll be some rain soon."

"I'm tired of the stories you make up to appease me and talk me out of what I know is true. When we get home, I never want to see you again. You have not helped me at all." Her voice grew louder. "And where's the screenplay? How many pages have you done? Why can't I see it?"

John couldn't help laughing. "When have you given me time to work on it? I'll be glad to leave, but who's going to be your bodyguard?"

Christina glared at him. She turned back to anxiously keeping an eye on the clouds.

—ᴡᴡ—

They arrived home in a downpour. The automatic garage door opener wouldn't work. "They're here. There's an alien ship nearby, causing electromagnetic interference."

John stifled a laugh. "The power's out, that's all, Christina. We'll have to make a run for it. Let's leave the bags 'til morning."

"Power outage caused by the alien ship! Let's go to a hotel!"

"Where's a hotel out here in the middle of nowhere?" He reached over and opened the glove compartment, pulled out a flashlight and opened his door. "I'm tired. I'm going in. You can come with me or sleep in the car. I don't care." Christina jumped out and ran behind him to the front door. He unlocked the door and went in. Christina followed and slammed the door and locked it. She stood leaning her back against the door while John found some candles and lit them.

"Are you going to stand there all night?"

"Check the house, John, all the rooms. Make sure there's no one here." He knew she wouldn't rest until he looked, so he went from room to room and gave them a cursory look, shining his flashlight around.

He came back and gathered her in his arms. "There's no one here but us, my love." Holding her, he caressed her hair until she relaxed.

———

John awoke alone. It was still dark. It wasn't like Christina to get up so early. He wondered what she was up to. He threw on his flannel robe and went to find her. She was at the kitchen table with her laptop and a cup of coffee.

Before he could say good morning, she blurted out, "I forgot to cancel my automatic payments to that effing sanitarium! Fortunately, I remembered before my bank sent them another payment."

"And good morning to you, too, Christina."

She got up from the table. "Sorry." She put her arms around his neck and said, "Good morning," and kissed him. Then she sat back down at the computer.

"Is that it?" John asked. Tuning me out for the day?"

"No, of course not. I'm looking for a house to buy. Do you want me to fix breakfast, or would you like to do it?"

"I can do it, if there's anything here to eat." He looked in the refrigerator. "We got eggs and cheese, equals omelets. And bread for toast."

"Sounds good."

While John was cooking, Christina found a house she liked. "Here it is!"

"Here's what?"

"The house for me. For us. Take a look."

"Duh, I'm in the middle of cooking your omelet. How about getting your laptop off the table and putting some silverware on it? And pour us some juice."

"Oh, all right." She did as he asked. He brought the food to the table.

"The only trouble is, it doesn't have a pool. I guess I can have one put in. And I don't like the color in one of the rooms."

"Do you think you can take a bite and tell me how good the food is before you start redecorating the house you don't own yet?"

"That's just it. I don't own it yet. I want to buy it today."

John shook his head in consternation. "You haven't even seen it! Just some trick photography on the Internet."

"Well, for seven million, it must be nice. Anyway, I'll offer six."

"Why do you want to move, Christina? You have a beautiful home in Larkspur."

"It feels too cramped. Too many memories. Too many ghosts. It's not private. They know where I live. Everybody knows where I live. It's too old. And it was my parents' house, not really mine. I want my own home. Something I choose."

"I guess those are good enough reasons. After breakfast we'll talk about it, get an agent. Right now, I just want to enjoy my breakfast. I had a long drive home, and I want to relax before you drag me around the countryside. You haven't told me yet if you like your omelet."

She took a bite, "Oh, it's fine. Wait'll you see this house! It's fabulous!"

After breakfast John asked to see the pictures of the house, but Christina said she wanted to surprise him with the real thing, so she got on the phone with the real estate agency which had rented them the house they were living in. She made an appointment for ten o'clock.

They met with the broker Ron Paxton, convinced him of Christina's ability to pay for a seven-million dollar house, then followed him to the property. It was an enormous two-story

French country style manor house. In silent awe, John took in the magnificence of the place as they walked from the car to the front entrance. The central section was two stories high with a pitched roof and a turret. The two sides were one story, also with pitched roofs. Several peaks and a couple of wide chimneys adorned the off-white stone walls. The windows and the doorway were slightly arched at their tops. A small balcony with French doors and arched shutters provided an overhang for the entryway of two large carved wooden doors said by Ron to be 18th century doors from France.

Inside were 8,000 square feet of fairy tale castle. Every room was a different color. Many rooms had peaked ceilings to match the peaks in the roof, with rustic wooden beams accentuating them.

They were standing in a large room with coral pink textured walls and excessively French 18th century furniture when John said in a low voice to Christina, "How am I supposed to write about an alien invasion in the 21st century when I'm living in this gaudy, overstated imitation 18th century French manor in the middle of nowhere in Sonoma County? It's too overwhelming."

"Shh," Christina replied.

They viewed the sunken tubs and double-headed showers, the low-flow toilets and the bidets. "This bathroom's bigger than my whole apartment," he whispered when they got to the master bath. They viewed the blue bedroom, the pink bedroom, the pale yellow bedroom, the professional kitchen with three ovens and chef's stainless steel six-burner range, a walk-in freezer and humongous refrigerator. They viewed the temperature-controlled wine storage room complete with hundreds of bottles of wine.

When they were done, John asked to speak to Christina alone, and Ron obligingly left the room.

"How many acres does this place have, Christina?"

"Fifty-three."

"How do you keep fifty-three acres secure?"

"The Homeowner's Association provides security. There are gates, cameras, a burglar alarm."

"Climbing a fence is easy, or how about landing a spaceship in the meadow behind the trees? How do you stop that?"

"I didn't think of that. I guess there's too much land to keep an eye on."

They asked Ron to show them something with less land. The next house was more suitable. It was a country manor style but less ornate, more Tuscan than French, two stories with bay windows. The exterior was a light gray with white stone trim, the living area walls were a yellowed parchment color, the bedrooms off-white.

Christina pointed upward. "Look!" A curved balcony extended out over the living room. On the balcony was a baby grand piano. "We can have a party and you can play for it from up there."

"And who are we gonna invite?"

"Oh, don't be silly. We'll meet people—our neighbors, country club members. This house comes with a membership to the most exclusive country club in Sonoma County."

"Let me show you the pool and spa," Ron said. "There's a pool house for weekend guests, and a nice little caretaker's apartment over the garage. Then there's the vineyard. The revenue from it can help pay your property taxes. And you also have an orchard with various fruit trees."

"How many acres have we got here?"

"Eight acres. Is that small enough for you?"

"That might be manageable," John answered.

Christina thought so, too, and they went back to Ron's office to write up an offer in the name of her trust. "I hope you can deliver the offer today, because I want to move in right away."

Ron laughed. "I can deliver the offer, but the owner has to accept it before you can move in. How soon can you get a cashier's check?"

"I could get one today. My bank has a branch in Santa Rosa. If necessary, we could drive down to Marin and get it directly from my branch."

"I'll call you when I get a response on the offer."

Christina got the call at seven-thirty that evening. The owner had written a counteroffer. It was a little higher than Christina wanted to pay, but she was impatient to move, so she accepted it. Ron came over with the papers and she signed them.

After Ron left, John wanted to know why Christina had bought the furnishings with the house. "You have all that beautiful furniture at your other house. What are you going to do with it?"

"I don't want it. Too many memories attached to it. I want to have everything new. A new life. I'll sell the house with the furniture. We have to get a broker in Marin or San Francisco." She paused a moment. "Maybe I'll keep it for a while to fool the aliens into thinking I still live there."

"What about your paintings?"

"I don't want them, either. They belong to my past life. Maybe I'll paint some landscapes here."

"What about your friends? Shouldn't you get back in touch with them now that you're out of the hospital?"

"My fair-weather friends? I don't want to have anything to do with them. My life has changed too much. Obviously, they have no understanding and very little feeling for me. Not only did they not visit me, but no one even sent a card!"

—⁓—

The next day they delivered a cashier's check for the balance owing on the property. Then they drove to Marin and got some boxes from U-Haul for packing up papers, books, clothing, and other personal items. Christina filled the boxes as well as several garbage bags. It was a somber occasion. They packed things up in silence, except for John's occasional questions about what she wanted to keep or give away.

Old photo albums seemed to disturb her. She wanted to throw them out, but John disagreed. "We'll just put them in the back of a closet. Later on you might want to go through them, and maybe they'll help me with the screenplay." Christina reluctantly agreed. When they came to her parents' bedroom, Christina started to cry uncontrollably. John put his arms around her and comforted her as best he could. "I'll take care of this room for you, Christina. Why don't you go pack up kitchen utensils and silverware and dishes. You aren't going to throw out that stuff, are you?"

"I don't know. Maybe not. I'll have to see."

"Is there a safe in this room?"

"Oh. I forgot about that. In the closet." The walk-in closet was about as big as John's apartment living room. Christina swung out a long mirror on hidden hinges over a cabinet of drawers and revealed a metal door with an electronic keypad. Christina pushed some buttons and the door opened to reveal several long narrow drawers. She turned away. "I don't want to look in there now. It's too upsetting. Just throw the things in a box and we'll go through them some other time."

After she left the room, John pulled open the top drawer. "Whoa!" He stared in amazement at the glistening diamonds, rubies, emeralds in necklaces, bracelets, earrings, brooches, watches. "She wants me to throw them in a box?" The next drawer held her father's watches, rings, and cuff links. Another drawer held a collection of old gold and silver coins, a few from ancient Rome. Two drawers held securities, and the last drawer held an assortment of thousands of dollars, euros, and pounds.

He decided to get some towels to wrap everything in. As he was leaving the closet, he noticed a rifle in a back corner. He made a mental note to get it later. He got some towels from the master bath, wrapped the items carefully in them, and put them in a packing box. He wrote "KEEP" in large letters on the box and carried it downstairs.

Christina was in the dining room staring at the dishes and crystal in the china cabinet.

"If I were a less honest man, Christina, and I knew a reliable fence, I could just take these valuables and disappear."

She looked him square in the eye. "You're not a less honest man and you won't leave me."

"Got me there."

The rest of the day was spent packing and sorting. What to keep and what to donate to her choice of charity, the Hospice Thrift Store. They threw out the spoiled food from the refrigerator, and packed up the canned goods. John looked at his watch. "It's too late to rent a U-Haul tonight. We should stay over, then move the stuff tomorrow."

"I don't want to stay here. They know this place, I won't be able to sleep."

"Nothing has really happened to you. They haven't killed you and if you were ever abducted, they brought you back, so I don't think anything's going to happen to you tonight, or ever. And anyway, just stay close to me in bed and I'll protect you."

Christina smiled. "Okay. As long as I'm with you, I can stay here one more night. I'll call out for some Chinese food."

"I'll light a fire in the fireplace and we'll get cozy. There'll be nothing to worry about."

They ate in front of the fire, then snuggled on the sofa. John fell into a comfortable bliss kissing Christina and fiddling lightly with her hair. His state of bliss was cut short as she suddenly piped up with, "Maybe that guy in Vegas found your car and put a GPS tracer thing on it so he didn't have to follow us. Maybe he knows exactly where we are."

"Oh my God!" John wailed in total frustration. She could always think of something to ruin their peace. Loudly, too loudly, he said, "He never saw us in our car! He wouldn't know which one it was!"

"Stop yelling! How do you know?"

"You ruined our blissful evening!"

Christina got up from the sofa. She turned on the floodlights and looked out the window. She went through all the rooms and looked out the windows. With the floodlights on she could see if anyone was approaching the house. Fortunately, she didn't see anyone out there. She came back to John.

"Well, did you see anyone?"

"No, but it doesn't mean they're not out there." Before he could reply to assuage her feelings, she said, "There's another safe in the library. Could you empty it for me?"

"Since our evening is ruined anyway, I'll do it." he replied. They went into the library. "All these books are still here! You haven't packed a thing in this room."

"Sorry. I just couldn't face it. Here, I'll open the safe and get you a box." The safe was built into the wall behind a painting. Not a very secure place, John thought. Any burglar would think to look there.

Christina punched in some numbers on the electronic panel and swung open the safe door. More documents, stacks of cash, a couple of gold ingots, three handguns and a few boxes of bullets. "Are those guns loaded?" John asked.

Christina shrugged. He checked each one, and had to empty each one. He put the bullets in the appropriate boxes. Then he unloaded the other contents of the safe into the box Christina had brought him.

"I'm not comfortable with transporting all these guns. Do you have permits for them?"

"No. I assume my father did. Look in the papers if you want."

"Why did your father have so many guns?"

"He kept them around in various parts of the house, for protection. After he died, I put most of his guns in the safe. I left a couple out."

"Yes, I remember the one you waved at me. Is that still upstairs in my room?"

"Maybe. Maybe I took it up to the rental house. I don't remember."

"Did you know about the rifle in the closet?"

"Oh, I forgot about that one."

"I'll get it later, along with several more boxes' worth of clothes upstairs. There's still so much to pack, because you didn't do much down here while I was working upstairs."

"Sorry. I couldn't do very much because it was so upsetting. So many memories I'd rather forget."

"I think you said that before."

"Well, maybe I did. I've lived here most of my life with my family, who are all dead now."

John didn't want to fall into the morbid thoughts of how she might have done them in, so he quickly swept her out of the room and headed for the den with the toasty fire.

—ᴠᴠᴠ—

The next morning Christina was looking at the stemware in the china cabinet. An empty box was waiting to be filled on the dining table, "I don't think I should put these glasses in the box without some cushioning. Get me some tissue paper at the drugstore to wrap them in. Some for the dishes, too. It'll be in the wrapping paper section."

"Don't you have some old newspapers you can use?"

I want tissue paper for these delicate glasses."

Yes, dear."

She turned from the cabinet to smile at him. "That's a married man's answer, isn't it?"

"Well, I'm beginning to feel that way with your issuing orders without even a 'please.'"

"Please get me some."

"Where's the drugstore?"

—ᴠᴠᴠ—

John packed Christina's parents' clothes in boxes, packing a separate box of expensive suits and ties he would like to keep for himself, as well as cashmere sweaters and a few shirts. Maybe if he left them in the back of his closet for a while, she wouldn't recognize them later on. If he asked about them now, she would almost surely say no.

The library was a more difficult matter. The room was filled with books, and John wanted to read some of them. He mulled over them for quite a while, selecting the most interesting ones. He filled a separate box with the books he wanted. Again, he figured he'd have to sneak them into his closet in the other house. He also set aside two of what he thought were nicest paintings to sneak into the back of his closet with the books.

He rented a U-Haul and filled it up with the items to be donated and took them to the Hospice Thrift Store as Christina had ordered. Fortunately, there were a couple of guys there to help unload the boxes. He got a blank receipt to fill out later.

He picked up some burgers and fries for lunch and brought them back to the house.

Christina greeted him and the food with a big hug. "How did you know I was starving?" She emptied the bags onto the table. "Burgers and fries? Not a very healthy meal."

"That's healthful, not healthy."

She glared at him. "Not only a writer, but a spoken-word editor, too."

"Advertising has corrupted the English language. There's no stopping the downward spiral into illiteracy, even though I try like hell to stop it."

"I didn't know you cared."

He put his arm around her shoulders. "I didn't mean you. You are one of the most literate people I know."

After lunch John said he was going to check out every room and make sure they hadn't forgotten anything.

He went upstairs and opened a door to one of the rooms he hadn't seen before. The furniture was covered with dusty sheets. John removed the sheets. Apparently the room had belonged to Christina's sister. Incredibly, all of her clothes, jewelry, books, perfumes, knickknacks, were still there, as if she'd never died. John called down to Christina from the top of the stairs.

She came up. "What's the matter?"

"Look in here."

"That was my sister's room. I don't want to go in there. I haven't been in there since she died."

"It looks like your parents didn't go in there, either. It seems to be the way she left it."

"Oh. I didn't know."

"Is your brother's room the same way?"

"I don't know. Probably. Could you clear them out for me?"

"Do I have a choice?"

She shook her head and went back downstairs.

He cleared the desk of papers and notebooks and put them in separate boxes. He intended to keep those to look at later, for any information about problems with Christina, UFOs, or any clues to their untimely demises.

He checked her brother's room, removed the sheets from the furniture. Untouched. He checked the guest room. Christina had taken care of that one. He brought up some more boxes and set to work. Then he packed up the clothes and loaded everything into the truck. He had to make another trip the thrift store.

When he came back, he loaded the truck again, this time with the things they were keeping. He put the boxes of items he wanted in the back along with the jewelry and other items from the safes. Then he loaded the boxes of things Christina wanted.

Christina followed him in his car while he drove the truck up north to their rental house.

She wanted to help unload the truck, but John insisted on doing it himself. He suggested she fix some dinner for them while he brought the boxes in the house. He stacked up most of the boxes in the guest room, making sure the ones holding things he wasn't supposed to keep were on the bottom. He stashed the boxes of valuables and guns in their bedroom closet.

"Well, that's done," he announced as he entered the kitchen. "What's for dinner?"

"Omelets again. We're just about out of everything but eggs and cheese. I hope you don't mind."

"Not at all. Are they about ready?"

"Coming right up."

John sat down at the table. Christina served him an omelet and whole wheat toast. "We've got orange juice. Want some?"

"Sure."

After Christina sat down, John brought up the problem of storing the valuables in the guest room. "I'll take you to your bank in Santa Rosa tomorrow and you can get a safe deposit box for the jewelry and stuff."

"Oh, they'll be all right here until we move."

"I don't want to take that chance. I'll feel more comfortable if they're some place secure. We don't have a safe or even a burglar alarm. It wouldn't take much for someone to break in here. This place is too isolated."

"Okay, okay. Just let me enjoy my food now."

"I want to use the pool house for an office, where I can work on our screenplay without interruption."

"You can't do that. You'd be too far away. I'll feel safer with you in the main house. You can have a room for your office, though. I won't bother you."

"Right," he said, not believing it for a minute.

13

It took three weeks for escrow to close and the deed recorded on the new house.

"You don't have to move all that stuff yourself, John. I'll hire a mover."

"It's not that much. I don't think you should entrust your extreme valuables to strangers. I can use the exercise. You won't go for walks in the woods with me, and you don't like it when I leave you alone and go by myself, so I haven't been exercising much. I'll get too flabby and you won't love me any more."

"Love you? Did I say I love you?"

"Not just now, but sometime you said it."

"I don't remember saying it. I don't remember you saying it, either."

"It must have been during the four days you don't remember."

"Just because I don't remember what happened during that time doesn't mean I lost my mind. Anyway, I remember quite a lot now."

"Why would you have to lose your mind to say you love me?"

"Oh, I don't mean it that way. I mean I was really burned by my last relationship as well as the loss of my family. I haven't been ready to get that involved emotionally. And I'm not ready to say that to someone who didn't say it first, or who I can't remember said it."

John mulled over the possibility of saying it now, saying that he loved her, but the truth was, he didn't know. Maybe it was just artistic lust and his feelings would fade after the film was made. He didn't trust her. He didn't want to be in love with her and find out later that she was a murderer. He wanted to try to resolve that question in his mind.

"I'm going to U-Haul now and get a truck." He kissed her on the cheek and left her wondering.

It was much easier to move this time. Most things were packed, and they didn't have all the thrift store stuff to deal with. Christina said he could have the library which was on the first floor for his office, but he said he wanted a room upstairs overlooking the vineyard. He said it was because of the view, but what he wanted was a closet to hide his purloined clothes and a place where he could lock the door to study the papers and books without her knowing.

—⁘—

They were enjoying the warm sunshine and pleasant breeze of April on the patio. "Well, how do you like living here, sweetheart?"

"I like it, except we have to have people coming on the property to manage the vineyard. And the maid service."

"They're the same people who contracted with the previous owners, so they're probably okay, not some new people who are aliens looking for you."

"I expect you to watch them very carefully. Maybe this house wasn't such a good idea after all."

"What do you mean?"

"Having a vineyard. Having too many rooms to clean. Needing help to do it. Remember the gardener in Marin. From a service I and my parents had used for years."

"I don't think your service actually sent him. I think he just made up a truck with their name on it. They would never have hired someone so incompetent. That guy was chopping up the flowers."

Christina smiled. "I think you're right about that."

John got up. "I'm going upstairs and get my room organized so I can get to work on the screenplay. What are you going to do?"

"Put away the dishes and silverware, I guess. There's really not much to do. Put my underwear in drawers."

"Can I help?"

"Very funny. You can help by calling the cable company. Have them hook up the TVs."

"Okay." He kissed her lightly on the forehead and went in the house. Christina sat there for a few minutes gazing peacefully out on the green hills. Then she looked up at the sky and realized she was alone, exposed out there, so she went inside.

John made an appointment with the cable company and went upstairs. He quickly hung up his clothes in the closet and looked at the boxes he had stowed there. He had been anxious to see what he could find in her sister's belongings that might give him a clue to whether Christina had killed off her entire family or not, but now that he had the opportunity, he would rather be writing the screenplay. He would look through the boxes another time. It was probably a dumb idea anyway. The police didn't seem to think she did it, why should he? Then he remembered the jewels and other valuables. He took the box downstairs.

Christina was putting the dishes in the china cabinet.

"Christina! We've got to put your jewelry in a safe deposit box."

"No, no. I've decided to have a safe put in the house."

"Fine, but you've have to have someone come in to install it."

She thought a moment. "Hmm, maybe not. They would know where the safe was. Maybe even how to open it. Okay, we'll get a safe depot box. Do we have to do it now?"

"Yes," John said firmly. "Let's go." So they went to the Santa Rosa branch of Christina's bank. Christina did not want to look at her parents' things, so John quickly put them in the deposit box, towels and all.

After that, they went back to the house and John sat out on the patio with his laptop to work on the screenplay. Christina wandered around the house a bit, familiarizing herself with the rooms and the furniture in them. Afterwards she went out to the patio and positioned herself in a chair across the table from John. She stared at him intently until he was disturbed by her presence.

"How am I supposed to get any work done with you staring at me?"

"I don't know."

"Don't you have something to do?"

"I'd like to rearrange some of the furniture with your help."

"Some other time."

"I can't think of anything else I want to do."

"You could go swimming."

"Not warm enough."

"You could bake some cookies."

"Now that's an idea. Only we don't have any flour, or sugar, or nuts, or chocolate chips. You know, John, I don't think we have much food at all around here. We should probably go grocery shopping."

"Can't you do that by yourself? I'll stay here and work."

"You think I'd go out in the car by myself, go into the store by myself. You think just because we've moved to Santa Rosa that I've changed?"

Wearily, John shook his head and shut down his laptop.

That day was pretty much wasted as far as John was concerned. They needed food, and they got it, enough food to feed several people over an extended period during possible natural disasters. Christina insisted he help her put the food away. It seemed to take forever to organize it all.

—␣ᵚᵚ␣—

The next morning after breakfast John set up his laptop out on the patio again to work on the screenplay. He got a whole paragraph done before Christina interrupted him. "We've got to get this place fenced," she said.

"It's already fenced."

"That white fencing with the diagonal boards is too low and you can see right through it. I want six or eight-foot redwood fencing."

"That's ridiculous. It's not going to keep extraterrestrials out, if that's what you're worried about. They've got eight acres to land a spaceship on."

"I guess you're right. What we need is a couple of big watchdogs."

John rolled his eyes and nodded. "Yeah, right. I'm going back to work now."

Christina went back in the house and left John alone for about half an hour. He was really getting into a writing flow when she came back out swinging his keys in her hand. He looked up. "What now?" he asked none too pleasantly.

"The dogs. Let's go get them."

"What? You're not serious!"

"I'm very serious. I looked up dogs on the Internet. Hundreds of breeds to choose from. I like Scottish deerhounds. I found a kennel with puppies for sale."

"Have you ever had a dog?"

"No, but now I can. We've got lots of room for them to run."

"It sounds to me like they'll be more interested in running down deer than aliens. Why don't you get a real watchdog, like a German Shepherd or a Doberman?"

"I prefer the milder temperament of the deer hounds. They're much more attractive, too."

John laughed out loud. "I'm sure the aliens will care that they're attractive."

Christina tisked loudly and handed John the keys. "I made an appointment. Let's go."

"You're the boss, even if you're wrong," he said as he closed his laptop and got up. He wished he could just walk out the door and never come back, but where would he find work? The piano? Maybe if he practiced up he could play in bars and restaurants. That had helped get him through college, why not make a living from it now? Of course it wouldn't be the living he'd been accustomed to. Barely enough to survive, probably, but it might be worth a try. He got into the car. He could really get away from her if he got a gig on a cruise ship. Cruise ships. "Ha!" he exclaimed aloud. They would do a background check… well, maybe they wouldn't find anything. More likely he was on a blacklist. But he'd start practicing every day. Have to go back to his apartment, get his

Fakebooks. Or, maybe some new books. And, or… He heard a voice.

"Come on. Stop staring into space. Let's get out of the driveway at least."

"Okay, okay." He turned on the ignition and started down the driveway. "Where are we going?"

"To see some dogs."

"But where? Which way do I go when we get to the main road?"

"I got a map off the Web. I'll give you directions as we go."

"You know, dogs will take up a lot of our time, and they'll want to sleep in our bed. I don't want them on the bed."

"Don't worry. I'm getting two dogs so they'll keep each other company and won't bother us as much."

"Sure they won't. You live in a dream world."

"I don't think I'm the only one."

The puppies were ten weeks old. Christina picked one up. "Oh, these are the sweetest things."

"Yeah," John said. "Real scary watchdogs. Gonna lick the shoes right off the burglars." Christina handed him the puppy. "You can't get puppies, Christina! A watchdog is full grown. It'll be a year or two before these mature enough to be any good."

"But they're so lovable."

The puppy was licking John's face. It made him smile. "Yes, they are, but trouble with a capital T, and, like I said, no good as watchdogs." He handed the puppy back to Christina. "I'm firm on this. No puppies!"

So they left the kennel with a crate and two yapping Scottish deerhound puppies in the back. Christina had seemed so happy playing with the puppies that he decided it would help keep her calm and her mind occupied to have them to take care of. In other words, he had caved in to yet another of her foolish whims.

The puppies were yelping and whining in the crate. Christina commanded him to stop the car. She got out and took the puppies out of the crate to hold in her lap in the front seat. They struggled to get away from her hold and succeeded, bouncing onto John's lap and climbing up his chest to lick his face as he tried to drive. He pulled over. "I can't drive like this, Christina. Put them back in the crate!"

With the face of a little girl about to cry from being scolded, she put them back in the crate and then plopped down huffily into the passenger seat.

Finally, they arrived home. John unloaded the crate, then the bag of puppy food. It was going to cost a fortune to feed these dogs when they were full grown. Fortunately, that wasn't his problem. Lastly, he unloaded the doggie bed big enough for two puppies to sleep together in on the floor. He knew that bed would not be slept in, at least not at night when he wanted them to. The kennel owner had told them they could put the puppies in their crate at night. They were used to a crate, she had said, and would feel safe and comfortable in there. He didn't believe the woman, and he knew it would be difficult to enforce that rule with Christina. He also knew he had to enforce it or say goodbye to their sex life.

He carried the dog bed into the house. Already the puppies had urinated in the foyer. They were nowhere in sight, and neither was Christina.

John took the dog bed up to the bedroom. Christina was padding the crate with bath towels. The puppies were wrestling on the bed. "I said I don't want the puppies on the bed!"

Christina stood up. "I didn't want them wandering off while I was fixing their crate. They're too little to jump off the bed, so I put them up there."

John put the dog bed on the floor and placed the puppies on it. They bounced off and ran around the room. One puppy stopped and pooped on the carpet.

"Shit!" Didn't you take these dogs outside yet?"

"I wanted to get things set up first." She cleaned up the mess with some tissue and went into the bathroom to flush it down the toilet.

John yelled after her. "You don't know anything about taking care of dogs, do you? Have you ever had a dog?"

Christina came back to the bedroom. "My parents wouldn't let me have any pets. They said they were too much trouble."

"They were right. What will you do with them when we go out?"

"They can go with us."

"What if we want to go on a trip?"

"They can go with us."

John picked up the puppies and went downstairs. Christina followed them. He took them outside to a grassy area and put them down. They nosed around and did their business in carefully selected places.

"Look, Christina. I have less and less time to devote to your screenplay which you were in such a hurry to get made and show to the world. Now there'll be no time at all. I'm not ready for children in this relationship. These puppies are worse than children. I don't have time to take care of them."

"I'll take care of them, John. I promise they won't bother you."

"Oh sure. Like you're going to come out here by yourself with the dogs. You're going to take them for walks by yourself. You're going to take them to the groomer by yourself or give them a bath by yourself. You're going to chase after them out in the field by yourself when they get away."

"The property's fenced. They can't get very far."

"They can crawl right under the fence or climb through it, and when they get bigger, they can jump over the fence. These dogs are one of the tallest dogs in the world when they are full grown. Can probably jump a six-foot fence."

"Then I'll build a seven-foot fence."

John couldn't take it any longer. He charged back into the house and grabbed his laptop and took the stairs two at a time up to his room where he shut himself in.

Since he met her, he had no control over his own life. None. Maybe he didn't have much control over his life before he met her, but at least he could go home after work and relax—alone if he chose. Most guys could get away from their wives or girlfriends' demands by going to work. He couldn't even do that now. He contemplated the possibility of working for a tabloid, making up outrageous stories for them. It was the antithesis of journalistic reporting, the lowest of low slimy jobs.

He e-mailed his resumé to the tabloids even though he knew he wasn't going to write stories about UFO landings or three-headed rats invading New York City. It would feed him a pinpoint of false hope for a while. He ordered a jazz Fake Book online, and then went to work on the screenplay. As soon as he got into a good scene, Christina knocked on his door.

"John? Are you in there, John?" More knocking. "We should walk the dogs," he heard in a muffled voice.

"Go ahead and walk them yourself!" he called back. "I'm working on our screenplay."

She jiggled the handle. "Let me in! I can't go out alone."

"You have your watchdogs. You'll be safe."

"Open the door!"

"All right!" He slammed his laptop shut and opened the door.

They put leashes on the puppies and went out for a walk.

"Have you thought of names for the puppies?"

"I was thinking Kayla and Kieran."

John's cell phone rang. He stopped and looked at the caller's number. It wasn't one he knew, so he let the voicemail take the call. While he was looking at his phone, the puppies were circling him, entangling his legs in the leashes. He put the phone away, took a step forward and fell over.

Christina laughed. The puppies attacked him on the ground and licked his face. John tried to be stern, but he found himself laughing, too. Christina knelt down and helped John sit up. She brushed him off a bit. "I'm sorry I laughed. You just looked so funny, I couldn't help it. Are you okay?"

"Yeah." He lay back down and pulled her down to him and started kissing her passionately. The puppies started climbing on them. John pushed Christina away and sat up. "Well, that didn't work." He disentangled himself from the leashes and got up, held out a hand to Christina to help her up.

They walked back to the house, John's arm around her shoulders and Christina's arm around his waist.

John brought his laptop downstairs to the family room sofa. "Christina, do you know anything about Scottish deerhounds?"

"Well, they're great hunters, especially for deer. Their parents were champions, so they're perfect puppies. They could be champions, too."

"Are you planning on showing them?"

"I don't think so. It seems like too much work."

"We'd better find out more about them. I'll Google them." John found a website about the breed. He scanned the page, shook his head. "Great! Just great, Christina."

Christina sat down next to him and peered at the screen. "What?"

"It says here they don't usually bark and don't make good watchdogs."

"Oh," was all she could think of to say.

"It also says they're difficult to train."

"Oh," again.

"They are loyal to their owners."

"Well that's something, isn't it?"

"Hmph," John replied. "You really need to take these dogs back. If it's watchdogs you want, we'll look at some other breeds."

The puppies were trying to climb up the sofa. Christina picked them up and put them on her lap.

She stroked the puppies gently as they fell asleep. "I don't want to take them back. I love them. They're so sweet."

14

Several days of attempted puppy training on John's part went by. The only thing the puppies learned was to go outside to do their business, which was perhaps the most important thing in the world. Along with that, though, were constant interruptions in his writing because the puppies wanted to play outside.

John called a carpenter to put in two doggie doors—one from the kitchen to the garage and one from the side door of the garage to the yard. He also called a fencing company to enclose about an acre for the dogs. This way they could go in and out on their own and not wander away.

When all was done, John showed the puppies the doggie door. He pushed them gently through the doggie door from the kitchen and then through the doggie door to the outside. The puppies caught on quickly, and immediately went back into the house.

His work on the screenplay was moving far too slowly. At this rate, he thought, if the aliens were coming, they'd be here before he finished.

"Christina," he said one morning, "I'm going to have to lock myself in my room for a while to get any work done on your screenplay."

"Go ahead. Just don't forget we've been invited to a cocktail reception this evening at the country club to welcome us to the community."

"How can I forget something you never told me about?"

"I did tell you, a week ago. You should wear a suit."

"Yeah, sure."

"A good one."

"Are you suggesting I'm too uncivilized to have a good suit?"

"No, I know you have at least one—the one I bought you in Vegas."

"What time is the event?"

"Seven."

"Did you ask about attire?"

"No. It just stands to reason. Country club, evening, cocktails, suit."

"It might stand to reason in San Francisco, but here seems to be less formal. I think people move up here to get away from all that."

"So you're not going to wear a suit?"

"Call them up and find out the suggested attire."

"I'm not your secretary, John," she said emphatically.

"I'm not your secretary, either. I'm your writer and your bodyguard. And dog handler."

"Wear a suit or call them yourself."

"That sounds more like it," he chuckled. "Got the number?"

It turned out that a sport coat, no tie, was sufficient.

"Ha, ha! Sport coat, no tie," he taunted. He gave her a quick kiss and ran up the stairs to his room.

Inside, he locked the door. Then he looked in the closet at his stash of boxes of Christina's unwanted stuff. He needed to do some research. He took out an old family photo album and propped himself up comfortably on the bed. He thumbed through the typical family life pictures, stopping especially at pictures of Christina. Christina, the new baby home from the hospital, Christina standing in her crib, mirthful with a twinkling smile. Christina riding her tricycle. Her first grade picture with a toothless grin.

It made him think. *There's something about discovering the child in the person you love. It just warms your heart to love them even more. LOVE?* He slammed the album shut. It was too late, though. He realized how much he was in love with her. Her tenderness toward the puppies had started it. Now he had really crossed over the line. And he knew there was no going back. It didn't seem so bad, after all—love. So what if she was crazy? At least she wasn't normal and boring. He felt he had enough of those traits for both of them.

He put the album away and went to work on the screenplay. He worked diligently for about an hour, until Christina knocked on his door. "It's lunchtime, John!" she called. "I've fixed a pasta salad. Come on down and get some!"

He knew he shouldn't leave his room. He'd get nothing done the rest of the day if he did. "Can you bring some up here? I'm busy working."

"Okay, but I miss you. I want to eat lunch with you."

No, better not."

In a few minutes she knocked again. "I've got your lunch."

He opened the door and she waltzed in with a tray of food and set it on the small table with two chairs by a window.

He looked at the tray as he sat down. "Hey, there are two plates."

"Yes," she smiled slyly as she removed the plates and drinks from the tray and stood the tray up against the wall below the table. She sat down and spread a napkin on her lap. "If you won't come to me, I'll come to you."

He had lost again. It wasn't a total loss, though. After lunch they made love, and then he fell into a luscious and dreamy afternoon sleep. He awoke refreshed. Christina was nowhere to be seen. He looked at the clock. Five o'clock! The day was practically gone. He didn't feel like working now. Maybe a cup of coffee would help revive him. He was aware, of course, that if he went downstairs, distractions could keep him from coming back up to work. He didn't know exactly what distractions yet, but he was sure they would involve at least three entities—Christina, Kayla, and Kieran.

John tried to sneak down to the kitchen to grab a cup of coffee. The second his foot hit the ground floor, the little "non-barking" puppies came running and barking at him. They tried to climb his legs.

"Off!" he said sternly to no avail. Christina joined them. "See, John? They can bark."

"I'm going to get some coffee and go back up to work some more."

"We don't have much time. The reception's at seven."

"I know, Christina. It doesn't take me two hours to get dressed."

"Before you go back up, can you go with me to take the dogs out for a few minutes?"

"We got them a doggie door so they can go out whenever they want."

"Yeah, but they only want to go out with one of us."

"Look, Christina. I'm getting nowhere fast on the screenplay which you thought was so urgent. The yard is fenced. You should feel safe going out there without me."

"Well, I don't, so you'll have to go with me."

He prepared a small pot of coffee and went out with them while it brewed. The puppies weren't interested in doing their business. They were only interested in wrestling and chasing balls. John had a bucket of balls. Every time he threw one, the puppies would run after it. They would fight over it, chew it, chase each other, but they would not bring the ball back. John threw ball after ball until all the balls were way out in the yard. Pretty soon the puppies were tired and lay down for a nap in the grass. They never did do their business.

"Okay, Christina, that's it. I'm going in now. I've wasted enough time." He picked up one of the puppies and took it in the house. Christina brought in the other one. "If they make a mess," he said to her, "you can clean it up. I'll be upstairs, locked in my room."

He took his coffee upstairs and sat down at his computer. Half an hour had passed. He only had half an hour left before he had to get ready to go. His cell phone rang. He looked at the caller's number. Not anyone he knew, but he decided to take the call anyway.

"Yeah."

A woman's voice queried, "John Davis?"

"Yeah. Who's this?"

"Alicia Frampton from *Exposed.* You sent us a resumé."

"Oh, yeah."

"We'd like to interview you and Christina Markham."

"I'm the one who's looking for a job, not her, and how do you know her name, anyway?

"We have our ways, Mr. Davis. Your story in the *Bay View* caught our attention, so we've been doing a little research. How did you enjoy your trip to Vegas?"

"How'd you know about that?"

"Like I said, we have our ways."

"Did you send a guy to stalk us in Vegas?"

"I don't know anything about that. We want to interview the two of you about what you wrote, find out truth or fiction." She paused, then, "I don't want to interview you for a job."

"Well, that's why I sent you my resumé, not to be interviewed and misquoted by your trashy paper."

"Trash sells. We're very successful. We're not interviewing you for a job because we know you can't be trashy enough."

"Thanks for the compliment, but we're not interested in being interviewed. It would compromise our credibility to the world."

"And what credibility do you have now, Mr. Davis, after trying to pass that story off as truth?" John pushed the button to cut her off. He shouldn't have exposed himself as wanting credibility. She might wonder why they wanted credibility, what they were up to. She might keep snooping around and bothering him, and Christina, too. He made a mental note to warn Christina.

Now he had to get ready for the reception. He quickly showered, shaved, and dressed, then he went to Christina's room. The door was open. She was just slipping on a slinky little black dress.

"Wow! You look marvelous!"

"Thanks, sweetie. I've got to get some jewelry on, and then we can go." She dug into her jewelry box and pulled out a diamond heart pendant packed with countless little diamonds and a pair of dangling diamond earrings. "Could you help me with this necklace?"

"Sure." He put it around her neck and fastened it while she put on her earrings. "You are a vision of loveliness," John said, gathering her to him. He bent to kiss her, but she resisted.

"I don't want my lipstick messed up. It's time to go. Later you can mess it up."

"What do you plan to do with the puppies? They won't like being alone. They'll probably chew up everything in sight."

"I can put them in their crate. They'll go to sleep."

"Don't count on it, Christina."

"Of course they will."

"It would help if we take them out for a few minutes and wear them out a little."

They took the puppies out for some exercise, then Christina put them in their crate. The puppies started whimpering when she closed the door on the crate.

"Ohhh," she said in sympathy.

John herded her firmly out the bedroom door before she could attempt to rescue them.

In the car, John told Christina about the call from Alicia Frampton.

"Why wouldn't I want to be interviewed? It would be my chance get my story in the papers, to warn people of what's coming."

"Because it's a paper that makes up stories. People like to read *Exposed,* but hardly anyone believes anything in it. They print trash, and if you're in there, whatever you say is considered trash. You come off as a nut case. It will not bode well for the future of our movie, for at least two reasons. One, your movie will be disregarded because the theme of it was published in *Exposed.* Two, somebody might steal your idea and make their own movie. It won't be as good as yours could be, but that's it, somebody made your movie and it's too late for you to do it. So…"

"So I should talk to no one about it, even tonight. I should not mention what I've seen or that I've been in a sanitarium."

"You got it. Even if you think the person you're talking to is harmless or sympathetic, someone else may be listening in."

"Okay, and you keep your eye out for people who look like they don't belong there, John. Especially alien looking ones."

"How can you tell?"

"I don't know—shifty eyed, or," she laughed, "people without navels, like that guy in Vegas."

"Oh, yeah, 'Excuse me, ma'm, may I look at your navel? I'm doing research on innies and outies.'" He tried to lift up her dress for a navel inspection. They both laughed.

"Not now. You can inspect it later." She pushed him away and straightened her dress.

—⁓—

They arrived at the country club. John was looking for a parking place. "You really must use valet parking, John. It looks like you're poor if you can't afford five or ten bucks for the valet."

"Yeah, yeah. Rich and infamous. That's me. Which reminds me, you don't have to mention to people about my news article or that I got fired. Don't even mention I was a reporter."

"What'll I tell them?"

"You can tell them I'm writing a screenplay, but absolutely no details about what. It's very hush-hush."

"Can I say that — 'very hush-hush?'"

"Yeah. Very clever of you. Adds a little intrigue. We'll seem less boring than we really are."

Christina did a mock pout. "You think I'm boring?"

They arrived at the valet parking area. John stopped the car.

"No, no. You're the most exciting woman I've ever met." He leaned over and kissed her cheek.

A white-haired man was checking membership just inside the door. Christina showed her card. "Ah, our guest of honor," he said with a British accent. "And who, may I ask, is your escort, Miss Markham?"

"This is my business manager, John Davis."

"Allow me to see his identification, if you please."

"Of course. John?"

Irritated that the man did not speak to him directly, as if he were not there, John stepped up to the counter and slapped his driver's license down in front of the man. "Here," John said curtly. The man took up the license and looked at it, then at John. Then he made a notation in the guest book on the counter. He turned the guest book towards John.

"Sign here, if you please. Name, address, driver's license number, and phone number."

John wrote down everything that was on his license, then he wrote a fabricated phone number. He turned the guest book back to the man, took Christina's hand and led her away from there into the milieu of cocktail sippers and finger-food nibblers. They approached the bar with some difficulty, as people were bunched up close to it. They all had drinks already. John wedged his way in to the bar and Christina after him as the people on either side made way for them, well, for Christina, at least. Two seats were empty so they sat down. The man next to her smiled and said, "You must be the new girl in town."

"Yes, I am." She looked at him briefly and then faced forward, looking for the bartender.

"Do you have a name?" the man asked.

Christina replied, "Do you?" She turned to John. "When you get the bartender's attention, I want Cinzano over with a twist of lime."

He leaned close in to her. "Okay, baby, anything you say. Finally, we're really on a date."

"Yeah. It feels good. I haven't been out in eons, except for the dinner you took me out for that I can't remember, so it's like we didn't go at all."

The bartender showed up and took their order.

Christina put her hand on John's arm. "The man next to me asked if I had a name."

"Did you tell him?"

"No, I asked him if he had one."

"Did he tell you?"

"No. I turned away before he could."

"I think you should be more friendly to your neighbors, otherwise they won't come to the housewarming party you're planning."

"I don't know if I want to have it now."

"Why don't you introduce us?"

"Okay," she said. She turned to the man on her left. He was looking at her. Christina smiled and held out her hand. He took it. "I'm Christina and," she motioned to John, "this is my fiance, John."

"Fiance?" John blurted out. "Oh, yeah, uh, John Davis." John reached across Christina and shook the man's hand.

"Bob Alexander. You look familiar. I've seen you somewhere recently, I'm sure. Are you some kind of celebrity?"

John chuckled. "Yeah, the notorious kind."

Christina didn't like feeling squeezed between the two men conversing. "John, they've got a beautiful grand over in the corner. Why don't you play something and liven up this party?"

"You play the piano?" Bob asked.

"Sort of."

"We could use some music around here. Nobody ever plays that thing. Let's hear something."

Christina nudged John up out of his chair. He headed for the piano, and she followed him. It was her opportunity to stop the uncomfortable mingling with strangers.

John sat down at the piano and dug into his mental repertoire for a tune appropriate to this pretentious gathering of conspicuously wealthy people —"Puttin' on the Ritz." When he started to play, heads turned, faces smiled at the welcomed diversion from the small talk. Christina stood next to the piano and lightly moved her body in time with the music. She started singing along.

John was so surprised Christina was singing he bungled a chord. She had a sweet, soft voice, and completely on key. He kept going. He didn't think he should say anything to disrupt her flow, so when he finished that song, he segued into another song he thought she might know and that might suit her voice, "Can't Help Lovin' That Man of Mine." She knew it! She sounded great. All she needed was a microphone next time. When that song was over, he stopped to talk to her. When he stopped, people applauded. Christina smiled and gave a nod to the audience.

"I had no idea you could sing! You're fabulous!"

"Oh, I can sing a little, but I think you're exaggerating."

"No, I'm not. We could get gigs! Have some fun."

"Aren't you supposed to be writing a screenplay?"

"Sure, but I can't do that 24/7. What else do you know?"

"I don't want to sing any more tonight. I'll have to practice. Can we go home now?"

Before he could answer, Bob Alexander came up. "That was great, Christina. Can you sing "Fly Me to the Moon?"

"Not tonight, Bob. We've got to go home so John can work on his screenplay."

"A writer, eh? What's it about?"

Christina gave the approved answer. We can't say." She lowered her voice to almost a whisper. "It's very hush–hush."

Bob laughed at the melodramatic way Christina delivered the line. "Tell me, Christina, is it any good?"

"It's good. It's going to be a blockbuster. It's a sci-fi suspense psychological thriller romance. That's all I can say."

"That covers just about everything but comedy."

"There's some of that, too," John added.

"You got a producer?"

"Not yet," John said. "We're looking. You know somebody?"

"I know people. Give me your card."

John didn't have any cards, but he felt around in his pockets as if he expected to find one. "I don't have one on me, but I'll give you my number."

"What's your background?"

"My background? MS, Journalism, Stanford, news reporting, features."

"Where?"

Christina took that as her cue to interrupt. She rubbed her forehead. "John, I'm getting a headache. I need to go home."

"Okay, sweetheart." He shook Bob's hand. "Good talking to you. I'll be waiting to hear from you about a producer."

The puppies started whimpering and barking when John and Christina came in the front door. Christina hurried upstairs to let the puppies out of their crate. John followed her up and headed to his office. He was excited to move forward on the screenplay now that he had some hope of getting a producer.

He no sooner turned on his computer than the puppies came bounding in, followed by Christina. "They were so lonely in the crate the whole time we were gone," she said.

"They probably forgot about us and slept the whole time. Puppies naturally stay quietly in their den and wait for their mother to return from hunting. It doesn't bother them unless they're really hungry."

"What do you know?" Christina responded with some irritation. "You're just too hardhearted."

"If I were hardhearted, I wouldn't be here." He got up and took her in his arms. "You melted my heart and now I'm hopelessly in love with you, but the puppies aren't as unhappy as you think."

She was going to argue the point, but he kissed her, and that was the end of the argument, and the end of his plans to work on the screenplay that night.

He started working in earnest early next morning after eating a bowl of oatmeal and some seven-grain cinnamon toast, and a banana. Christina was as anxious as he was to see the screenplay finished. She left him alone and kept the puppies out of his hair until lunchtime. She even went outside with the puppies by herself, but she stood close to the door in case something threatened her.

—〰— *15* —〰—

Two weeks went by, during which time John finished the first draft of the screenplay, gave up his apartment in the city and brought the rest of his stuff home to Santa Rosa. He had enough money saved up to buy outright a decent mobile home, and scrape by on his own if he ever wanted to move out, so he was feeling less trapped and more secure. Living with Christina finally felt like home to him. Since she had the puppies to keep her busy and had renewed her interest in music, she had calmed down a lot. She let John work on the screenplay with little interruption.

John had invited Brad to come up for the weekend, and he showed up on Friday afternoon. Christina sequestered herself upstairs while John answered the door. "Hey, Bradley, come on in. Good to see you."

Brad didn't notice John's usual play on his name of Bradford. He was too busy gawking at the splendor. "Wow! I don't know what else to say, man. You've got Heaven here. This is an incredible place!"

John smiled. He led John out to the patio. "It has its drawbacks. Dogs, for one. Or for two, to be exact. They're a nuisance sometimes."

"Woe is you, poor boy."

"Then there's the pool, the vineyard people, decorators, maids, gardeners. I have to see to everything. Christina doesn't like to deal with strangers she think might be sinister aliens from other worlds."

"Could be worse, John Boy. You could be livin' on the street without gainful employment." Brad nodded his head as he looked around at the view from the patio where they were standing. "This looks pretty gainful. When do I get to meet the vision of wealthy loveliness?"

"Maybe dinnertime. She's upstairs wondering what planet you're from. Have a seat and I'll get us a couple of beers."

Brad sat down at the patio table. At that moment, the two large puppies bounded out of the house and tried to climb on him. "Whoa! Hey, there, pups." He ruffled their fur, moved them down onto the ground, but they popped up again.

Christina came out the door. "Kayla! Kieran! Off!" She pushed at the puppies until they got down. "Sorry. They're still learning." She held out her hand to Brad. He took it in his and shook it gently, held it a moment.

"I've heard so much about you. Glad to finally meet you," Brad said.

"I hope you only heard the good stuff," Christina replied.

"Oh, yeah. John is always telling me how beautiful and sweet you are, and," he stole a glance at John, "how crazy he is about you."

"That's it? He didn't tell you I'm insane and have an alien fixation?"

"What? Of course not."

John broke in. "Brad and I were thinking of playing golf tomorrow, Christina. You don't play golf, do you?"

"No, but I might come with you and watch, if you don't mind." She glared at John. In a very even, restrained tone, "You never mentioned playing golf tomorrow. You know I don't like being here alone."

"Well, I'm mentioning it now."

She wasn't buying the idea that they go without her. "We could go wine tasting, the three of us, instead. We haven't done that yet."

John shrugged his shoulders. "I'm a prisoner of love. What do you think, Brad?"

"About the prisoner of love bit? I could give it a try if I found the right woman."

"No, the drinking."

"Oh. Yeah, drinking's good, but you're the entertainers. Up to you guys. I'm just here for the food."

Christina decided. "I think we should go wine tasting, then have lunch at the Korbel Champagne Cellars. I was reading about it the other day. It's not far, out near Guerneville. We really haven't done any sightseeing since we moved here, John. It would be fun."

"What about the dogs?"

"We could take them with us."

"No! They'll only be in the way, and we'd have to leave them in the car while we go into wineries. They wouldn't like that."

"You could get a puppy sitter," Brad suggested. "Or take them to doggie daycare." He was joking, but John picked up on the idea.

"I'm going to Google doggie daycare, see if there is such a place. Would that be okay with you, Christina, if I find a place?"

"Sure. That's a great idea. Thanks, Brad, for the suggestion."

John went in and Googled "doggie daycare" and found a place. He gave them a call. Then he grabbed three beers from the kitchen and headed back outside.

"All set," he announced. "Doggie Daycare will take them off our hands tomorrow."

John gave Brad a long walking tour of the property, beers in hand, while Christina hung out close to the house with the dogs.

John brought up the subject of a producer.

"I did get a referral for one," Brad said. "I tried to get hold of him, but he's in Scotland on location for his latest film. He won't be back for a couple of months."

"I met a guy over at the club who says he knows people."

"I've heard that before, Johnny. Don't hold your breath. Guys are always trying to impress with that line."

"Yeah, but I'm going to keep on him, try to make him come through on it. Here we have the fruit orchard. Apples, plums, walnuts, other stuff."

"This is quite a spread. Are you going to marry her?"

"Maybe. I don't know. She's not quite normal yet."

"What makes you think she'll ever be normal? It doesn't happen. Anyway, if you decide not to, let me know. I'll marry her. What a looker!"

"Don't get any ideas, Bradley."

The next morning they dropped the dogs off and headed west on River Road for Korbel. Pastureland and vineyards quickly gave to way to redwoods and the bushy undergrowth one sees near rivers. "This looks pretty remote," Brad remarked. "Are you sure this is the right way?"

"Yeah," John answered. "Haven't you been out of the city before?"

"Oh yeah, but never out here. I've been to wineries in Napa and Sonoma. They're a little more civilized looking."

Korbel was housed in a picturesque old building fronted by a huge parking lot which detracted somewhat from its charm.

They decided to skip the tour and went to the cafe for lunch. They ordered their sandwiches and sat on the patio under the trees. Brad said, "So, Christina, what's this screenplay about that you and John are writing?"

"Don't you read your own newspaper?"

"Ah. That's the story line then?"

"More or less. John's doing the actual writing. He says you might know someone, a producer who might be interested."

"I did find one, but he's in Scotland for the next couple of months, and I don't know if he's even looking for something. They're leery of letting writers send them stuff. They don't want hundreds of bad screenplays in their mailbox."

"Ours isn't bad," she countered. "Are you still thinking of that rough scene that the idiots at your paper saw fit to print on the front page?"

Brad smiled. "Oh, is there more?"

"Very funny, Bradley," John said. "If you'll sign a nondisclosure agreement, I'll let you read what I've got."

"Is that what our friendship has come to—signing nondisclosure agreements? You think it's so good I'd want to steal it?"

"I doubt you'd steal it, but because I'm working for Christina, it's part of my job to get things like nondisclosure agreements."

"Then I'll sign on the dotted line. You're right to protect your intellectual property. That's the way it should be done."

"I'm glad you're not offended."

"Oh, but I am. This is going to cost you a bottle of champagne later to assuage my feelings."

"Assuage your feelings?" Christina laughed. "Do you journalists always talk that way?"

"He's just trying to impress you with big words, Christina. Don't let him fool you."

"I only talk that way when it'll get me a very expensive bottle of champagne."

After lunch they went to the tasting room and tasted the wines offered. Then John bought two bottles of champagne, one for Brad and one for him and Christina. Then they picked up the puppies and went home. John downloaded a nondisclosure agreement, filled in the blanks, made a few changes to the contractual wording, printed it out and Brad signed it. "If I have any useful criticism or suggestions you can use, do I get paid for this review?"

"Of course," John replied.

"I don't suppose I can take it home and read it there?"

"No. You have to read it here."

"Are you going to barbecue tonight? A big fat steak would be tasty out here in the wilderness."

John laughed. "Yeah, I was planning on it. New York steak, baked potatoes, salad, garlic bread."

"Okay, but I'll be too busy to help you figure out how to light the grill, ha, ha."

"A simple matter, I'm sure. I think I can manage without you. Help yourself if you want a beer."

"Thanks," Brad replied, and took the manuscript out to the patio to read.

Meanwhile, John took up the issue of golf with Christina.

"It's not like you haven't been left alone before. Right after I met you, I went to my office. You were safe while I was gone."

"Maybe that time, but you never know when they'll show up."

"Look. I've gone everywhere with you, moved you, babysat you, took you to Vegas where we had no fun at all, put up with the dogs. I manage your property, and so on, and so on, and so on. Now on Sunday Brad and I are going to play golf down at the country club. You can stay here or hang out at the club, go swimming or whatever, but I want a day off, and I'm taking it."

Christina stared at him, a hard look in her eyes. "What do you want—a raise?"

"Yes, but don't change the subject. You've got an alarm system here. I'll be only minutes away. I'll have my cell phone on if you need to call me."

"I guess I can't stop you," she said, "but you'll be extremely sorry if something happens to me while you're gone."

"It's more likely something could happen to me, like getting hit in the head by a golf ball, than anything can happen to you here." Christina turned away and disappeared somewhere into the vast cavern that was the house. John shook his head and mumbled, "Why me?"

Christina was still in hiding when it was time to fix dinner, so John started without her. He prepared a salad and his homemade salad dressing, washed some asparagus, took the steaks and baking potatoes out to the grill, which was not far from where Brad was sitting. He stared at the grill for a moment, opened it up and looked in, closed it again. He looked at the dials, the knobs, the gas pipe and slowly shook his head. He stole a glance at Brad, who, rather than reading the screenplay was watching him intently.

John smiled sheepishly at Brad, then headed for the door. "Back in a minute."

Brad called after him, "What I thought! You don't know what you're doing! Better not ruin my steak!"

John ran upstairs to find Christina. She was propped up on their bed writing in a notebook. "I thought of some more things you might need to know for the screenplay."

"Oh, good, now that I'm finished with it," he said. "Do you know how to start the grill?"

"Uh, no. You got a manual?"

"It's your grill. Where's the manual?"

"I don't have a clue. Why don't you ask Brad?"

"Can't do that. I'm a male. I'm supposed to be born with barbecue expertise."

"Well, sorry about your mutant genes. I'm a woman. I have no ego. I don't mind admitting I know zero about the grill."

John went down to the kitchen to look for the grill manual. He was rummaging through the drawers when he heard a knock on the open kitchen door. He turned. It was Brad, grinning widely.

"Need some help, Johnny? Want me get it started for you?"

"Yeah. Christina said I have a mutated gene which prevents me from knowing how to start it. It's not my fault."

"Do you know how to cook steak and potatoes on a grill?"

"Is it different from the broiler?"

"After you wash the potatoes and pierce them with a fork, cook them for about five minutes in the microwave, then wrap them in foil. Get the garlic bread ready. Apparently I'm going to have to do the cooking if I don't want my steak ruined. Just watch and learn, John Boy."

"Okay by me, Bradley. I had no idea you could cook."

"There's a lot you don't know about me."

Like what else?"

"Like I like to be introduced to wealthy women, so if you know another one, keep me in mind."

"Christina and I are going to do a musical act down at the club soon. You can come and look for women yourself."

"Hey, I'm for that. What instrument to you play, the comb? Oh I forgot. You never comb your hair."

John quickly smoothed his hair back with his hands. "That's not true. I combed it before you came over."

"Yesterday?" Brad looked John's hair over and laughed.

"I play the piano. It got me through college. Christina's got a great voice. We just have to do some rehearsing."

Brad fired up the grill and John got the steak and potatoes together and readied the garlic bread. When the food was almost ready, he called Christina down for dinner. The puppies, of course, ran ahead of her, nearly tripping her on the stairs.

Christina sat down at the patio table. John came out wearing a knit cap. Christina and Brad laughed. "What's that?" Brad asked. "The new style chef's hat for beginners?"

"This is how I foil alien attempts to read my mind." He took off the cap and pulled a piece of foil out of it.

Brad laughed. They wouldn't find anything worthwhile in your brain. Why bother?"

"Amen to that," Christina said. "You're marking fun of me, aren't you? I don't like it a bit."

"No, no. I was just making a lighthearted joke, liven the party, you know, like the proverbial drunk who wears a lamp shade on his head?"

"Oh, I see," Christina said. "Too much beer. Where's the plates, the silverware, the napkins?"

John put his hands on his aproned hips in mock indignation. "I can't do everything. Surely you can do something like that."

Christina got up. "My name's not Shirley," she quipped. "Brad, he's making it sound like I can't do anything. Really, I can cook."

"It's true, Brad. She can. Sorry, Christina. I was just feeling a little peevish because you were upstairs lounging around while we guys did all the work."

Christina looked at the several empty beer bottles on the patio table and the barbecue table. She gathered up the bottles. "Yeah, it looks like you were working very hard." She took the bottles into the kitchen, brought out the dinnerware and napkins, and set the table. Brad brought over the food.

They no sooner sat down than John jumped up in feigned alarm. "Christina! You forgot the ketchup!"

"No, I didn't. I didn't think anyone would want to ruin these beautiful steaks with ketchup."

"Well, I wouldn't, either," Brad said. John headed for the kitchen. "Hey, John, bring some steak sauce while you're at it!"

"Didn't you make an *au jus* sauce?" Christina asked Brad.

"No, because the steaks are already jus' right."

John returned with the ketchup and steak sauce. He sat down and poured some ketchup on his plate.

Christina continued. "I prefer *au jus* sauce on steak. Of course I prefer chicken to steak. Less fat and cholesterol."

John stopped cutting into his steak to wave his knife. "Man is a carnivore. He needs his steak for energy."

"For what? To go hunting in the forest for more steak?" To Brad she said, "It's delicious, Brad. You can cook for us any time."

After dinner Christina cleaned up while Brad looked over the screenplay with John watching him intently for his reactions. After a few minutes Brad looked up. "I can't concentrate while you're staring at me. Why don't you and Christina go practice some songs?"

"What do you think so far?"

"So far, interesting. That's all I have to say for now. Now go!"

John went. He and Christina worked on putting a musical set together for a couple of hours. Then Christina said she was tired and went to bed. John went out to the patio to see what Brad had to say about the screenplay.

"That girl has got some voice!" Brad said.

"Yeah, what about my screenplay?"

"I've made some notes about the weak and boring parts. Here." He pushed a stack of pages toward John.

John thumbed through them. "You've written all over these pages! It can't be that bad!"

"Just some suggestions. I don't claim to be an expert, but I watch a lot of movies. I think it needs more excitement. Less of the everyday stuff. Loading the dishwasher, cooking an omelet. Going to the grocery store. Come on. We get that in real life. We don't want to watch it in a movie."

"You don't know anything!" John retorted.

"Well, I know when I'm bored."

"It's not an action film! It's a romance, a psychological suspense."

"Where?" Brad asked with a teasing twinkle in his eyes.

John started to take the rest of the pages from him. Brad slapped down his hand on them to stop him. "All right, all right. I'll lighten up. You wanted my honest opinion. That's all it is. An opinion. Just let me read the rest with the right type of movie in my mind. Most of it's good. I'll pretend I'm watching it with a girl. This is going to appeal to girls more than guys."

"I'll leave you alone, Bradley. I'm going to head up to bed. Lock up when you're ready to come in. And don't stay up too late. We're teeing off at nine."

"Okay. See you in the morning."

Christina did not come downstairs for breakfast or see them off. She told John she had gotten very little sleep the night before because she was anxious about being left alone while they golfed. She wanted to try to go back to sleep.

John took the puppies out for a few minutes and then fed them their breakfast. He and Brad had breakfast at the country club before starting their round of golf.

John thought it was going to be great to be away from Christina for a while, but she called him so many times in the first hour that he lost count.

"This is getting ridiculous," he said to Brad. "I'm turning off my phone."

"It's about time you did," Brad said. "Is this what she's like all the time?"

"No, because I hardly ever go out without her. The day I rescued her from the sanitarium I went out alone and it was my last day on the job. She called me at the paper with some story about an alien digging in her trash, interrupted my screenplay writing. You know what happened after that. I'll call her in about an hour so she doesn't get totally freaked."

"Oh, yeah. That was in the screenplay. So this is your real life you're writing about?"

"More or less. Let's get on with the game."

When John called Christina later, she didn't answer. "Now what? She's not answering her phone."

Brad offered his opinion. "She's probably getting back at you for going out without her. If you get worried enough, she thinks, you won't leave her alone again. I wouldn't react to it."

"I'm not running home to see what's up. Maybe she's just in the shower." Still, he worried about her the whole time. It put him off his game, and Brad won.

When they got back, the puppies were loose in the house and came bounding out of the living room to greet them. Christina was not with them. John looked in the living room. The puppies had made a mess of it. Torn up magazines were scattered about on the floor. Sofa pillows likewise. One of John's shoes was on the sofa with Christina's cell phone.

"Christina!" John yelled out a couple of times. No answer. They searched the house for her. John took the stairs two at a time to look in their bedroom and in the bathroom. Not there. Brad looked in the yard and out by the pool. John called the club to see if she'd walked over there, even though he was pretty sure she wouldn't go walking alone. Christina had not been seen at the club, either, so John and Brad got in the car to check the road to the club. Nothing. They drove back, past Christina's house. About a mile up the road, they spotted her walking very slowly in the middle of the road, in the opposite direction from the house.

John pulled over and jumped out of the car. He ran over to her. "Christina! What happened? Where are you going?"

She stopped and turned to him. She had a vacant stare in her eyes, as if she was hypnotized. She said nothing.

He gently shook her. "Christina!"

She then seemed to come to her senses. "What? John." She looked around. "What are we doing here?"

"You were walking out here by yourself. We've been looking all over for you. Are you all right?"

"I don't know. I was in the living room with the puppies. I heard a strange noise outside and went to the patio door to look out. That's all I remember."

"Let's get in the car." Brad had been waiting in the car so John could talk to Christina alone. Now he got out and got in the back seat. Christina still looked a little spacey, so John didn't say anything until after they were home and in the house. He led her to the sofa and sat her down.

"I'm going to get you some water. You stay put." He brought her a glass of water, and she drank about a quarter of it slowly, then handed it back to him. Brad figured she'd feel more comfortable talking about the incident if he wasn't there, so he got a beer out of the fridge and went out on the patio with it.

John sat down next to Christina and put his arm around her. "What time is it?" she asked.

He looked at his watch. "It's almost one."

"Missing time. I noticed the time when I went in the living room. It was ten-thirty! I must have been abducted, but I don't remember anything."

"It was probably like last time, when you didn't remember four whole days. You didn't get abducted then. I was with you then, the whole time."

"That's just it, John." Her voice became strident. "You weren't here today to protect me. They saw their opportunity, and they abducted me."

John sighed. "I still don't think you were abducted. You're here, and you're okay, aren't you? Not hurt anywhere?"

Christina got up and left the room, John calling after her, "Christina! Wait!" She didn't stop. She ran up the stairs. He heard a door slam.

John straightened up the living room and went out to the patio where Brad was. "Sorry, man. She's holed up in the bedroom. I don't know when she'll come out again. The downside of living with Christina."

"So you don't think she was really abducted by aliens?"

"No. I don't think anyone has been abducted by aliens. I have a theory that some abductions may have happened, but they're done by the government surreptitiously testing people for genetic damage from radiation exposure."

"But it's been decades since the nuclear bomb tests."

John paced back and forth in front of Brad as he talked.

"And abduction reports have been going on for decades. I think now they're testing descendants of people who've been exposed. And the cattle mutilations were also tests to see how continued radioactivity in the soil was affecting cattle. Look where the mutilations were reported. As for the highly developed surgical instruments said to be beyond our technological ability, they probably used laser scalpels, not beyond our ability at all at the time as ufologists said. Whatever "new technology" introduced to the public has probably already been around awhile in military R&D. It's all very convenient to have the public think aliens are behind everything."

"Maybe you got something there. You should write about it."

John stopped pacing. "As if the government isn't after me already."

"So are you thinking the government is also implanting mind control chips in these abductees?"

"Only a few questionable anomalies have been found in purported alien abductees, so I don't know. Could be in the testing stage. It's just too hard to imagine they would really do that."

Brad thought a moment. "Maybe it's not the government *per se,* but some agency within that is operating covertly, on their own."

"This is getting to sound too much like a sci-fi thriller. Let's can it and fix something to eat. Christina probably won't come down any time soon."

"Well, your screenplay, as it is, is pretty good. But it's fiction. Why don't you write what's really going on?"

"Brad, what IS really going on? I don't know!"

"Write what you think, and see what happens."

"Are you wanting me to get myself killed? Because whether the government's involved or not, they are not going to like the implications."

"Right now they think you're writing about extraterrestrial activity. They'd be happy with that. Goes along with their cover-ups. They won't know what you're doing until your film is released to the public. Then what point will there be for them to get rid of you? If something happens to you after that, the public would figure it was their doing, a belated attempt to silence you. The government wouldn't want that. I think you'd be safe. They would just deny, deny, and deny, as usual. Anyway, there's stuff all over the Internet along the lines of what you've been saying. More likely they'll ignore you."

"Who the hell knows? You're screwing with my plans, and my head! This movie was supposed to be about aliens trying to take over the earth! Can we forget it for a while and eat?"

"Sure, but when do I get my check for reviewing your manuscript? Is Christina gonna come back down soon?"

I doubt it. I'll pay you and get it from her later. How much you want?"

"Is five hundred too much?"

"No. You're worth it."

John got his checkbook, made out a check and handed it to Brad. "Thanks, man. What's for dinner?"

"Leftover steak." They made steak sandwiches out of a leftover steak, then Brad headed back to the city.

John wished he'd taken more classes in psychology. Maybe then he could deal with Christina better. Better yet, maybe he would have understood himself as well as her in the beginning and never responded to her letters. He could be just going about his old life the same as always. Some parts of his life now were interesting and amenable, such as sex, the house, the grounds, the golf course, the Steinway and a partner who could sing. The screenplay was a very large plus, the first real creative effort he'd been able to complete and feel satisfied with.

His relationship with Christina was at times blissful and satisfying in many ways, but also frustrating. He wished she'd get over her paranoia. If, as Brad suggested, she was trying to manipulate him by pretending to have experienced missing time because of her fear of being alone, he'd like to know how to put a stop to that. However, he wasn't sure Brad was right. If she was so afraid, why would she intentionally walk out by herself onto the road? Wouldn't she stay locked in the house as she'd done before?

Before he could speculate any further, Christina came downstairs, the puppies charging ahead of her to jump all on John. "Hi," she said.

"Hi," John said back. "Are you feeling better?"

"Yes. I don't seem to have any aftereffects from the abduction."

"You mean the missing time. You don't know if you were abducted if you can't remember anything."

"Let's practice some songs," she said. John smiled a wry smiled. There it was, the old "change the subject" routine whenever he hinted she might be wrong.

"Sure." He went over to the piano and sat down. "We should get some music for songs that you want to sing. Our repertoire is sort of limited."

"It will do for now. Maybe tomorrow we can go to a music store, or… do you think we could find some on the Internet?"

"Probably. You wanna look now?"

"Could you look for me? You're better at that stuff than I am."

"Okay. Let's do it." He got his laptop and they sat down together on the sofa. He found a website where he could download sheet music and pay for it with a credit card. They picked several tunes and he downloaded them. Then they went upstairs to John's office, puppies underfoot, where he printed out two copies of each song.

They went back downstairs to the piano and rehearsed for a couple of hours, then it was time to eat. Christina fed the dogs while John scrounged around in the refrigerator and the cabinets for something to make a meal out of. Christina was not into cooking much. Her idea of cooking usually involved sandwiches, salads, or eggs—something quick and not too involved. He imagined that she didn't get much practice growing up in a wealthy family. She wasn't into housekeeping, either. They probably had maids and a cook.

John found a frozen lasagna, frozen green beans, and frozen french bread, so he set about defrosting the bread, microwaving the lasagna, and cooked the green beans on the stove. He also made garlic bread and heated it in the toaster oven.

Christina let the puppies out and stood just outside the kitchen door to the patio while they did their business. Then she came in and put silverware and wine glasses on the table and sat down to wait for her dinner. John put the food on the table when it was ready. He found a bottle of Zinfandel, opened it, and sat down across from Christina. He poured the wine and they filled their plates. John took a couple of bites of lasagna, washed it down with some wine, then ventured to break the long silence. He wanted to try to find out just what was up with the so-called abduction.

He spoke rather slowly, tried to choose his words carefully to avoid a backlash. "Uh, Brad wondered if you made that up about the abduction to keep me close to home in the future. I said I didn't think that was the case."

Christina looked away, didn't say anything for a moment. She appeared to be thinking. Then she looked at John and said, "I wonder if they are trying to wipe out my memory banks so I won't remember being abducted. So I won't remember any of my experiences related to them. So I won't remember what they're up to, but it's not working, because the only things I can't remember are what they do when they've got me."

He was amazed she didn't get angry at him for suggesting she was making things up. Was this a kind of changing the subject while appearing not to because what he said was correct? "Where's there?"

"Their spaceship, I guess. Where else?"

"I don't know, Christina." He had a few more bites of food, took a sip of wine. Christina did likewise. "What do you think of the possibility that it is not aliens at all, but some secret government agency that is abducting people and conducting tests for radiation exposure?"

"What radiation exposure?"

"Ongoing exposure to fallout from nuclear tests. It might even explain the cattle mutilations. And what about people who claim aliens took their eggs or sperm? Testing to see whether mutations had occurred due to the exposure?"

Christina stared wide-eyed at him. "Oh my God," she uttered in almost a whisper. Then she shook her head a little. "It doesn't explain the implants."

"Well, those could be to track the people they tested. A lot of people said they were abducted more than once—many times, even. How would they know where they were to abduct them again? Probably many had moved. Maybe they want to test them throughout their lives to see the effects. And," he added, "they want to avoid an uproar from the public about the exposure which most people have forgotten by now."

"But why would they test people who weren't alive during the bomb tests? Who were born much later?"

"I've thought about that. Maybe they want to see what effect it had on the offspring of contaminated people. What mutations occurred, what the children's chromosomes look like. Also, the radiation is still in the soil. How much of an effect is it having today? UFOs are a great cover-up, Christina. When was the first major UFO report?"

"Nineteen forty-seven? Oh! Just a couple of years after the atomic bomb was invented, tested, and dropped on Japan!"

"You got it. I think they started planning this so-called research way back then. Planned the UFO diversion. It was useful in more ways than one. When they tested new military aircraft, and when they started testing people. They couldn't put in tracking chips then. That came later."

"What you say sounds so plausible, John, but it doesn't explain the transformation, the animal-like furry people hanging on hangers. You're just trying to talk me out of what I know!"

"Maybe your dream was symbolic. They're kidnapping us and testing us without our permission. We're just lab rats to them, or chimpanzees!"

"That's scarier than aliens! If that's the case, what can we do about it!"

"I can't prove anything. It's all conjecture. If it's true, what could we do anyway?"

"Couldn't they just get the information from doctors' records, hospital records?"

"Maybe people weren't willing to cooperate. Or there was too much chance of being exposed with so many knowing what the government was up to."

"It's the mind control thing that worries me," Christina said. "It was in my dream. People seeing things that weren't really there. Accepting it as normal. How do you explain that?"

"I can't believe it. It's just too sinister. I can't believe the government would try to control our minds that much. But there may be some people, some agency in the government who would like to, or at least experiment with it. I've heard of some experiments, ostensibly to control our enemies."

Christina got up and started clearing the table. "Do you think they're planning to control everyone's minds someday? Oh, I just thought of something—my dream of being in the 1940s."

"More possible symbolism pointing to the nuclear tests. Your subconscious was trying to point to that time period." John laughed.

"What's so funny?"

"I was just thinking, you said you had large breasts in the dream. Big boobs, big bombs."

"You're very logical and can make all the pieces fit your theory, but it's wrong! I don't want to talk about it any more!"

"Okay," he said. "Just think about it."

They cleaned up the kitchen in silence, then went outside with the puppies. They stood together, looking up at the stars, Christina nestled in John's arms. John was admiring the beauty, Christina was looking for UFOs.

"The stars are beautiful tonight," John said.

"Mmm," Christina replied.

"You feel a little tense. Relax, enjoy the view."

"It's hard to do. I keep wondering if there's a UFO coming after me."

He turned her around and looked in her eyes. "This view is even better," he said and kissed her.

The next morning Christina surprised John with a demand to read the screenplay. She had previously shown no interest in reading it or participating in the writing or structuring of it. All she had done was give him bunches of notes, often disconnected, about her experiences, dreams, and weird thoughts. He had assumed she trusted him to write the story satisfactorily. He thought it was finished and ready to go, but knowing how changeable she could be, he just might have to start all over with it, and have a lot of arguments with her in the process. It was, therefore, with much reluctance that he handed it over.

"Remember when you read it that I'm a professional writer and I think I know what angle will interest people. It may not fit whatever vision you may have about it, which vision you never relayed to me other than you wanted people to be aware of what might happen."

"We'll see, John," was all she said about it, and took the manuscript out to the patio with her coffee. "Could you fix breakfast while I read this?"

He mused over her sudden interest in reading the manuscript as he whipped up some pancakes. "Oh, I get it," he muttered aloud.

"What?" Christina called from the patio.

"Nothing! Just talking to the pancakes."

Of course. It was my bringing up alternative reasons for the UFO phenomenon and abductions. She wants to make sure that's not in there. Why did I do it? He sighed and poured the pancake batter onto the griddle in six blobs.

Christina kept reading through breakfast, which meant John had to clean up the kitchen afterwards. When she finished reading, she gave him her opinion.

"It's not like I imagined it would be, but I like it. You've written our story here. It's takes on almost more importance than the invasion."

"And…?"

"And I like it. There's just a few things I think you should bring out more, I made some notes on the manuscript."

John look over her notes. "You have some good points there, Miz Markham. I'll work them over."

"Just one more thing, John. The scene where Jesus descends on a cloud at the White House. How do you know it's going to happen like that?"

"I don't know. It just came to me in a flash." He laughed. "Maybe I'm Jesus, and I know everything."

"No, you're not. But I know who you really are now!" she said excitedly. "John the Revelator, who wrote Revelations! Oh, WOW!"

'It's just the logical way it would happen, if it were going to happen, which it isn't really. What other way could he convince people he was really Jesus?

"I think you were chosen like me, you just don't know it. Someone gave you that information and you wrote it out."

It was pointless to argue with her. "Whatever you say, my dear."

The phone rang. It was Bob Alexander, the man they'd met at the club who claimed to know "people." Bob had a producer for them to meet, so John made an appointment to meet at the club over lunch.

When he told Christina, rather than being happy and excited, she fired off a bunch of questions all at once. "Who is he? What does he do? How long has he lived here? Does he even live here? Is he a member of the Club?"

"Whoa. Slow down. You're right. We should find out about him. I'll call the association and see if he lives here. If they'll tell me anything. Otherwise, we'll see what he says when we meet up with him. This is why we should get to know more of our neighbors. Somebody could tell us something."

He called the association office. The woman who answered said, "We don't divulge information about our members. If you want to know something, you'll have to ask them."

"Sorry, Christina. She wouldn't tell me anything. When we go over to the country club for lunch, we'll ask. Maybe they have a roster of members they'll show other members."

They arrived early so they could ask about Bob.

Christina approached the white-haired, British-accented man at the desk who had been rude to John the night of the reception. "Hi, there."

"Yes, madam?"

"I'm Christina Markham, one of your members. Tell me, is Bob Alexander a member here?"

"I'm sorry, Madam, I can't divulge that information. You'll have to ask him yourself."

"Very well," she replied. "Thanks for nothing." To John she said, "Let's wait at the door, see how he gets in here."

They sat down on a sofa facing the door to wait. They had been waiting about ten minutes past the time of their appointment when Bob Alexander came around the sofa from behind, "There you are! We got here early and got a good table on the patio."

Startled by Bob's unexpected method of arrival, John and Christina jumped up from the sofa.

Bob motioned to his companion. "I've brought Eliot Denham here. Eliot, this is the lovely Christina Markham and her partner, uh, uh, sorry, I've forgotten your name."

"John Davis."

"I've heard of you," Eliot said. "Weren't you with the *Bay View?*"

"Yeah."

Eliot nodded his head slightly. "Interesting,"

"Shall we go to our table?" Bob suggested, and they followed him outside to their table overlooking a beautiful pond.

John ordered a bottle of wine for them. Expensive wine was one the more positive perks of his job.

Eliot ended their brief conversation about the beautiful weather with a "Did you bring your screenplay?"

"No, I didn't. I want to find out who you guys are first, your screen credits and so forth. I've never heard of you. Bob, do you live in this uh, development? Do you belong to the country club? No one here will tell us anything."

Bob smiled. "Yes and yes."

"Sorry to ask, but can you prove it to me? Give them permission to tell us?"

"Sure. I can do that. I completely understand your reticence. No need to apologize. On the way out we'll take care of it."

"How do you earn your keep?"

"Investments, deal making. Over the years I've accumulated so much money that I don't have to work now, but I still like to be involved in interesting projects such as yours."

Christina asked Eliot, "Eliot, do you have some screen credits we can look up?"

"Of course, Christina. I came prepared," he said as he handed her a presentation folder. "You'll see that I've produced or co-produced several feature films and documentaries. I started out with independent filmmakers and worked my way up to a hugely successful feature film for one of the top motion picture companies."

"Hmm," Christina mused, perusing the neatly typed resume. She closed the folder and handed it to John, who took a brief look.

"We'll go over it later." He set the folder aside and picked up his menu.

They chatted amicably over lunch, John telling of the events that led to the publishing of a rough draft of a personal work and subsequent firing, having the big three government agencies after him. They already knew about the incident, so it was something he might as well tell.

Eliot shared a few humorous anecdotes about the difficulties of working with big stars. All in all, they had a very enjoyable lunch, and Christina was feeling a little more comfortable with the two men. Nevertheless, she still wanted corroboration from the association that Bob was a resident, and they got it after lunch. All that was left was to check out Eliot Denham's credentials.

"At least they don't look like aliens," Christina said after they got home. "See what you can find on the Internet about Eliot, and Bob, too."

John got his laptop and started looking. He found several of the credits listed in Eliot's resume from independent sources. He was satisfied with the results, but Christina wasn't. She wanted to see a picture of Eliot on the Internet, but John couldn't find one.

"Anyone can find that information and print out a convincing resume," she said. "I want you to hire a private detective to find out what Eliot Denham really looks like. I would feel a lot better if your friend Bradford had found someone, instead of this stranger we met at the country club. Bob might not be who he says he is."

John shook his head in dismay. "Do you want to wait two months for Bradford's contact to get back, and then hope he doesn't have something else to do?"

"I'd be willing to wait for someone I could trust more. Maybe we could meet him now where he's working and talk to him. Find out where he is. We could arrange to hire him when he gets back."

"You're impossible!" With that, John stormed out of the house. He had to go for a walk, no, a run. He used to run regularly. How many years ago was that? He got winded early on and slowed to a walk. Out of shape. He would make it a daily practice from now on. To hell with her if she didn't like it!

His outing gave him a chance to go over his thoughts about the screenplay. The idea that the whole UFO thing was a cover-up by the government to mask their secret activities. He'd like to put that in his screenplay, yes, HIS screenplay. She didn't write it. Only part of it was even her idea—her delusion, that is. He would put his views in there, too. He wondered who was behind it all. Was it extraterrestrials, or was it the government or some rogue agency in the government? Let the viewer wonder, too!

When he got back, Christina was in the kitchen stirring something at the counter. He came up behind her and put his arms around her. "What are you making there?"

"Brownies." She hadn't baked anything since he'd met her. He had no idea she was capable of such a thing.

"My favorite food group. When will they be ready? Can I have some?"

"Of course. They'll be ready in thirty minutes."

"Where did you learn to make brownies?"

"It's not rocket science. Anyway, when I was a child, I often hung out in the kitchen with our cook, especially when she was baking goodies. I learned a little from her."

"When will they be ready?"

"I just told you. Thirty minutes."

"Can I have some?"

"Of course, silly."

I'm going to take a shower. Let me know the minute they're done."

The minute the brownies were out of the oven, John sat down with a glass of milk and took his first bite. "Mmm. Walnuts, too. If you're trying to assuage my feelings with food, you succeeded. This is pure domestic bliss."

After they had their chocolate fix, John broached the subject of a producer again. He didn't want to start a fight, but it had to be settled. "This Eliot, he can put two and two together and figure out that what he read in the paper is part of our story. If we don't sign with him, he might just make a movie based on that idea."

"It's not much of an idea, just one scene. How would he know the rest of it? His movie wouldn't be like ours."

"Come on, you know it would ruin our whole plan. You can't use the same scene in two movies, especially that one. I planned to flash back after that scene to the events that preceded it, then return to the scene and the finale."

Christina tried to object. "I'm not sure that's the way to do it."

"How do you know? You didn't even bother to read the damn thing until it was finished!"

"Well, I made more notes you didn't bother to read."

"I was already finished! I don't need any more information!"

"Stop yelling," Christina yelled. "Meet with Eliot. Get him to sign a nondisclosure agreement. Tell him we're still thinking about it, we're not ready. Why didn't you get one when we met with him?

How stupid!"

"You didn't suggest it at the time, either, so you're just as stupid!"

"Do I have to do all the thinking around here?"

John had to laugh at that one. "All the thinking? You don't do any thinking! And you don't do anything else around here, either, but make work for me to do. I can still get an agreement. Say we want to interview him in more depth. Get it at the start, and then actually interview him. You might change your mind if he can talk about his work intelligently."

"I don't want him!"

"Don't be so closed-minded. You don't know what he's really like. You're letting your paranoia judge him without a chance to prove himself."

It came as no surprise to him that, rather than agree with him, Christina disappeared into some other part of the house.

He was left with cleaning up the mess from the brownie orgy, but he didn't mind. He took inventory of the food supplies. There was chicken, there were steaks, there was hamburger meat, there was fish, but everything was frozen. He didn't like defrosting meat in the microwave. It never seemed to work right, and once he even got sick from eating chicken that had been improperly thawed. He opted for the hamburger meat. That was one thing that would thaw quickly in a skillet if he broke it up. He would make some spaghetti.

The most pigheaded woman I've ever met! A quiet, soft-spoken woman, that's what I want, but I'm not sure there are any these days. He minced a clove of garlic. At least she doesn't make me eat tofu.

They got off the plane at Edinburgh Airport at ten-thirty in the morning after a very long trip with little success in sleeping on the plane. Try as he might, John had not been able to persuade Christina to hire Eliot Denham as producer for her film. And it was her film. Her money, her story, and her paid screenwriter. So, they had traveled thousands of miles to reach this cold and dreary piece of the British Isles. There was at least a certain rugged, windswept beauty he admired on their descent. He liked to be out in the elements once in a while, properly bundled up and walking briskly to keep warm. He wondered how the inhabitants kept from being depressed living their lives out in a cold, damp place where it rained about half of every month and the average high temperature of the year was 63 degrees.

The weather in San Francisco was no piece of cake, but at least he could look forward to a few balmy weeks in the fall. The thermometer might even hit ninety occasionally in October. And on many days the fog lifted around noon, even though the breeze off the Bay required a sweater at the very least. If he wanted more warmth and sunshine he could get in his car and head north or south for less than an hour to find more pleasant weather.

John had objected strongly when Christina wanted him to carry a pile of cash. She gave it to him anyway. On the way to the airport he stopped at a branch of his bank and deposited most of it—after having to explain at some length to the manager why he had so much cash.

They stood in the customs line for quite a while, but once it was John's turn, it only took a few minutes. It took them a lot longer to look through all of Christina's luggage and examine her gold and diamond and ruby and emerald pieces of jewelry and fill out forms swearing they were for her personal use.

When she was finally finished, she joined up with John. "Why did you bring all that jewelry?" he asked. "You never wear it at home."

"Precisely why. We're going to be staying at a castle, an expensive one. I want to look the part of a wealthy heiress, which I am, of course."

"You're not one any more," he said teasingly.

"What do you mean?"

"You already inherited. That part is over. Now you're just wealthy."

"I'm not so sure. I think, once an heiress, always an heiress."

"I'm beat. Let's get the car and get to our bed." They had reserved a car for John to drive, because although Christina could well afford a driver, she wouldn't have anyone drive but John. John was grateful she did at least rent a very cool car—a silver Jaguar sedan.

"This part of the trip is going to be fun," he said as he turned the key in the ignition.

"Don't forget to drive on the left side of the road in your excitement, John."

He had forgotten, but he wasn't going to admit it. He would have to stay focused to keep remembering to drive on the left.

The sky was overcast, but fortunately it wasn't raining. They could enjoy the fertile green fields of the countryside as they traveled the hour and a half to the castle. It wasn't quite as bleak as John had imagined. Life flourished in this cool, damp clime. No need to irrigate here.

They arrived at the gated entrance of the private drive, where a gatekeeper checked their passports against the guest list, and then they drove through. They couldn't see any castle yet, The drive was lined with flowers and shrubs, with green lawns behind those.

"Wow!" John suddenly exclaimed. "There it is! That's a castle, all right, turrets and all. You picked a good one, Christina."

"Yes, it is beautiful, isn't it," she replied, pleased with herself. Is this like the home of your ancestors?" she asked. Does this country feel familiar?"

"No, why should it? I've never been here before."

"They say there's a genetic memory. Many people who visit a place where their ancestors lived feel they've been there before."

"Well, I don't."

"Maybe it's the wrong part of Scotland."

"I wouldn't know."

"Are you sure you're Scottish?" Scots aren't usually blond and blue-eyed, are they? Maybe you're adopted."

"No, I wasn't adopted. My mother has blond hair. Her mother came over from Norway. Anyway, there's probably lots of blond Scots."

When they pulled up to the entrance, a footman in traditional costume awaited them and took their luggage.

They entered the enormous high-ceilinged, wood paneled entry hall with a majestic staircase curving up on one side. A cheery middle-aged Scotswoman in contemporary wool sweater and skirt greeted them and checked them in. "Will you be dining with us tonight?"

"Yes," Christina replied.

"Dinner is at eight. Andrew here will show you to your suite." Andrew was a young man standing by their luggage. John insisted on carrying one of Christina's suitcases because he thought there was too much for Andrew to carry upstairs by himself. They followed him up the winding staircase past old portraits of people, names now unknown, from days of old.

"Wonderful!" Christina said when they entered the front room. "Look at that huge stone fireplace! And they already started the fire." I can almost walk in, it's so large."

"Well, see that you don't," John said. He tipped Andrew and shut the door after him. "This all seems a little extravagant, even for you. I'm a frugal Scotsman, after all, and although I see the need for a Jaguar, I don't see the need for this theatrical, uh, whatever you call it, waste of money."

"Don't try to spoil my fun, John. It's none of your business what I spend."

"It will be when you run out of money. How will you be able to afford me?" He helped her off with her coat. "Don't forget to write this trip off as business on your taxes." She took his hand and pulled him toward the bedroom. "Let's check out the accommodations."

The bedroom was as large as the front room. The focal point of the room was the large four-poster bed with curtains tied to the posts. Christina untied the curtains so that they hung down on either side of the bed and at the foot, creating a cozy hideaway. She kicked off her shoes and crawled in.

"What are you doing?"

"Come and see."

John opened the curtain. She pulled down the covers, lay down and patted the bed for him to join her. He removed his shoes and climbed in.

"It's kind of chilly in here," he said.

Christina pulled the covers over them and snuggled up to him. "We'll warm it up."

———

They slept most of the day and awoke to John's alarm clock that he had set so they wouldn't miss dinner. Dinner was not a formal affair but Christina wanted to wear her formal jewelry. She managed to blend her slightly ostentatious diamond necklace, bracelet, and earrings with a simple sleeveless black dress and a delicate, silvery Chanel shawl for an overall less formal look. She wore her hair down, carefully arranged to expose her dangling earrings. She looked simply elegant. Heads turned and eyes stared as she and John were ushered to their table.

She had created a little buzz in the restaurant—murmurs and an audible "Who is that?" She had also created frowns from two women less thin and elegant looking than she.

John looked at the wine list. "I was thinking of having some Scotch, since we're in Scotland."

"No. Champagne before dinner is the only way to go in a place like this, unless we go to the bar before dinner for a drink. Please, John. You can have Scotch whiskey another time. Do you know how long it's been since I've been out to dinner?"

"Yes. Just a few weeks ago in Las Vegas."

"That hardly counts. That alien man was watching us the whole time and ruined my dinner, ruined our trip."

"He was probably a reporter from *Exposed*."

Christina ignored his logical suggestion.

"Before that there was dinner in Monte Rio."

"I don't remember that, so it's like it never happened."

John ordered the champagne, Laurent Perrier Brut NV for £49.95. It wasn't the most expensive bottle, but he liked the description: Elegant and fresh with hints of citrus. "By the way," he said, "Isn't champagne a dessert wine? Should we be having it with our dinner?"

Christina glared at him. "We're having it before dinner. You can order another wine for the *entrée*. Anyway, I want champagne." End of discussion. They studied their menus. "Everything sounds wonderful. It's hard to choose. She settled on a lemon sole and John ordered venison from a nearby estate.

"What time is our meeting tomorrow?" Christina asked.

"I told you three times already. Why can't you remember?"

"Alien brainwashing, I guess. Come on, when is it?"

"We're meeting for drinks at a pub in the village at noon. He said he has about half an hour he can spare us. You know, Christina, he sounded a little put out that you didn't want to wait until he's finished with this project."

"Time is of the essence, my dear. It's important that we get this film made quickly. And, I didn't want him getting tied up with something else before we could sign him."

"The screenplay's not even finished yet."

"I thought you finished it days ago."

"It was, but you gave me more notes, plus some things happened that I wanted to incorporate. If you want it finished, don't give me any more notes or do anything weird."

"Weird? What have I done that was weird?".

John laughed out loud. People turned to stare at the person who had disrupted their quiet, expressionless dining.

Christina and John hadn't eaten since the airplane breakfast early that morning, so when the waiter brought the first course of smoked salmon on a bed of cucumber salad, they devoured it hungrily and waited for more. They were able to savor their *entrées* in a more leisurely fashion after the edge of their hunger was relieved by the first course.

The next morning after breakfast they took a leisurely drive to the village where they were to meet with the producer. They stopped for a walk along the hills above the coast. As Christina got out, she noticed that a black car pulled off the road and stopped a couple of hundred feet away from them. No one got out. It was a little foggy so she couldn't tell the make of the car.

"Look, John! Someone's following us!"

John looked in the direction she pointed. "Just someone wanting some fresh sea air like us."

"Then why haven't they gotten out of the car?"

"I don't know. Maybe they're making a phone call."

"How can you protect me if you aren't even paying attention to our surroundings?"

"Like this." He put his arms around her and kissed her.

She pulled away. "Not funny or romantic. You just want to shut me up."

"Not true. I want to enjoy your kisses every chance I get. These surroundings stir my passion for you, Please let me hold you and kiss you so we can remember this moment on the beautiful coast of Scotland forever."

She acquiesced, but kept her eye on the black car the whole time they were kissing.

"Shall we walk now?" he asked.

"No. Not with that car there. Let's move on towards the village. Maybe they have shops we can browse in."

"You mean hide in. Okay."

They got in the car and entered the roadway. Just before they rounded a curve, John looked in his rearview mirror. The black car was following them. He hoped Christina wouldn't look back, but she did.

"See? They're following us."

"It's just a coincidence."

"I saw a strange man on the plane. He was staring at me. I bet he followed us over here."

"I'm sure there were several strange men staring at you. Who wouldn't, you're so beautiful. How would you know which one was following us? And why didn't you mention it on the plane?"

"I hoped I was wrong. Can we ditch him?"

John laughed. "What is this, a spy movie?"

"I'm serious. We shouldn't let him follow us to where we're going."

"This is the only road to the village, Christina."

"You could speed up."

"If he's following us, he'll just speed up, too."

"At least then he'll know we're on to him."

"Look, whether he's following us or not, he's staying way back and not threatening us, so can we just finish the drive in peace?"

"I wish I'd brought my derringer. You should carry a gun, John."

"Yeah, like they were going to let me carry it on the plane."

"You could have put it in your suitcase."

"You're crazy."

"You're mean."

They drove the rest of the way in silence, John checking the rearview mirror frequently, Christina turning around to look out the back every minute.

They arrived in the village well ahead of time. John pulled up along the curb and parked the car. The black sedan which had been behind them drove on ahead. John tried to see who was in the car, but the windows were too dark. The car stopped half a block up the street at the curb, but no one was getting out.

"They weren't following us, see? They went on."

"Well, they stopped just up there, and they're not getting out."

"We'll wander around the shops awhile. I'm sure you'll like that, Christina. And then we'll see if there's an alley where we can enter the pub through the back. If anyone's following us, it's best they don't know where we're going or who we're meeting,"

"So there is someone following us,"

"I can't be sure one way or the other. It could be anybody, a reporter, the CIA, or ..."

"Or aliens."

"I thought they only drove space ships," John said facetiously as he opened the door. He got out and went around to Christina's door and opened it. "We'll browse the shops and see if the same person keeps popping up in every shop."

"Or hanging around outside," Christina added.

They started with the nearest shop, a woolen shop. John picked up a heavy wool pullover. "I could use a good wool sweater, especially here."

"The color is good for you. Why don't you try it on? I'll keep a lookout."

John took off his coat and current sweater and slipped on the new sweater. He looked in the mirror. "It looks good, don't ya think?"

Christina didn't take her eyes off the door to look at the sweater. "Yes, it does. Get it."

"You didn't even look at it, but I'll get it anyway. See anything you want?"

"If you'll watch the door, I'll look around."

"Sure. Did you see anyone get out of that car?"

"Nobody got out."

John looked out the door, up the street. The black car was still there. Christina tried on a pullover sweater. She went over to John to show it to him.

He glanced at her. "That's looks nice on you."

"Yeah, but it's scratchy. Wool makes me itch. I don't think I'm going to buy anything." She pulled off the sweater, then put her coat back on. "I'll watch the door while you pay for your sweater."

He paid and they left the shop, walked slowly up the street in the direction of the black car, ambling along as if they were tourists seeing the local sights.

Christina didn't let up about being followed. "I don't know how we're going to keep them from knowing where we're meeting the producer. Do you think our home is bugged? Our hotel room? Maybe they know exactly where we're going. Maybe they already planted a bug at the pub."

"I doubt it. Someone might have an interest in what we're doing, if they're up to no good. Some rogue agency. But how would they get in to plant a bug at home? We were nearly always there."

"Not true. We went out to the store. We went out to the cocktail reception. We went out to lunch to meet that producer. If they were watching the house, they'd know when we were gone. They would also know their way around burglar alarms."

"Anyway, they wouldn't know where we're going to sit, so I doubt if any bug has been planted in the pub."

They went into a quaint little book shop. "They still haven't gotten out of the car," Christina said.

"If they know where we're going, they don't have to until we get there. Or it's just a coincidence, and they're busy making cell phone calls. If we leave here through a back door and enter the pub from the back, we won't be able to watch the car to see if they get out. I vote for just walking in the front entrance. All this cloak and dagger stuff is ruining our trip. Nobody's following us. Let's just forget it and enjoy ourselves."

"Sure," Christina said. "I know you're really thinking someone's following us."

"Let's pretend they're not. What would they do to us anyway?"
"Kill us."
"Stop it!" John said too loudly.

The male shopkeeper asked in a strong Scottish brogue, "Can I help you with something?"

"No," John answered, nodding toward Christina, and with a wink toward the shopkeeper, "Women. They're always changing their minds."

The shopkeeper smiled. "You're right about that."

John kept an eye out the door while Christina perused a bookshelf. She picked out a book and paid for it.

"It's time to meet Mister 'Right,'" John said. They went out onto the sidewalk. "I got the directions and address. It's just up the street on the right."

"You mean where our follower is parked?"

"Yep, but don't you worry, little darlin', I'll protect you," John said with a cowboy drawl.

They crossed the street. John tried to sneak a peak into the car as they entered the pub, but he could still see nothing.

Eric wasn't there yet. They sat down at a table where John could see the car. Christina looked at the menu. "Strange food. I don't see anything I want to eat. We should have met in a restaurant or a tea room."

"We can go somewhere else later and eat. I'll order us some ale. Oh! There's a man getting out of the car!"

"He's coming in! What'll we do?"

"Don't do anything. Just sit here."

They watched the man as he came in. The man looked around, then his eyes stopped on John and Christina.

"John Davis?"

"Yes."

The man sat down and held out his hand. "Eric Dawson."

"Oh!" Christina exclaimed a little loudly. "Oh," she said again, laughing a little and exchanging glances with John, who wasn't laughing. She'd sucked him into her paranoia again, thinking someone was following them for nefarious purposes.

John shook Eric's hand. "Glad to meet you. We noticed your car behind us on the way into town. Are you staying near the castle?"

"I'm staying on the grounds there, in a cottage. I don't have much time. Did you bring a synopsis and the screenplay?"

John looked at Christina, who he thought had brought it. "Sorry, John, I left it in the car."

"I'll run down and get it, Won't be a minute."

Christina didn't know what to say to Eric while they waited for John. She smiled.

He spoke first. "So what's it about?"

"It's about a woman who's had strange dreams and experiences. She's seen the future. Aliens are coming to destroy our cities and transform us into furry playthings. Oh, that sounds very silly, doesn't it? It's really not as silly as it sounds. Better wait for John. I'm no good at talking about it."

"I hope he has something better to convince me with to work on it. I have a reputation for good films. I'm careful about the projects I choose."

John returned with the manuscript. "Here's a nondisclosure and the synopsis," he said, handing them to Eric.

The waiter brought them a round of ale. Christina took a drink, nearly choking on it.

"You okay?" John asked.

"It's warm! Awful!"

Eric laughed. "You'll get used to it."

"I don't want to," she replied.

Eric signed the nondisclosure agreement and handed it to John.

They sat silently while Eric read over the synopsis. Christina looked a little anxious when a man in a black raincoat came in and sat down at the table next to them. He stared at them, his face hard, unyielding.

Christina squirmed. John noticed. She tilted her head in the man's direction.

John looked over at the man, nodded to him in a faint greeting. The man did not acknowledge John. Instead, he picked up the menu and looked at it.

John looked at Christina and shrugged a little.

"Let me see the screenplay," Eric said.

John handed it to him. Eric read the first two pages. Putting it in his briefcase, he said, "I gotta go. I'll contact you in a day or two, let you know my decision." He got up from the table.

John got up and shook his hand. "Thanks, Eric."

The man at the next table was taking it all in. Christina was noticing he was taking it all in. As soon as Eric left, she wanted to get out of there.

Once outside, she said, "That man was watching us. He was scary looking."

John didn't answer. He was trying not to get caught up in her imaginings again, He would, however, keep one eye out for the guy in the future.

They walked down the street to their car. John looked back as he opened the door for Christina. The man was standing outside the pub. He was watching them.

John found a tearoom that served lunch. They had something to eat, then drove back to the castle.

They took a walk around the grounds before going in. Christina was worried about the puppies, "I hope the puppies are all right at Doggie Daycare. I'm glad they took them for an extended stay."

"I'm sure they're fine. Do you want to call and talk to the puppies? Find out if they miss you?"

"Very funny. Yeah, maybe I should," she teased.

John stopped and put his arms around her. "Maybe someday we'll come back and get married here. It's a very romantic place."

"I haven't agreed to marry you."

"Well, I haven't asked you, either. Maybe next year I will, or the year after that. But there is something I want to do now," he said leaning into her lips and kissed her.

"Let's go in now and see if they made the bed," she said.

He said, "Then we can mess it up again."

———

While they waited to hear from Eric, they found several things to do to entertain themselves. They toured castles and churches, and spent a day sightseeing and shopping in Edinburgh. John wanted to take a hike along the rugged, windswept moors. "I don't think so, John. It's cold out. And too much open space."

"Come on. I'll bundle you up. You can wear my new sweater." He brought it over and started helping her into it like one would a child. "There we go. Now here's a hat to keep your head warm. You'll be okay."

They set out across the castle grounds. "I like to imagine what it was like for the people who lived here in more primitive times," John said. "What it was like to live closer to the elements. If we walk far enough, we'll be away from civilization, isolated, as the early Scots must have been."

"Oh. Your ancestors. They must have been a hardy people, to survive these conditions."

"Yes. Do you know anything about Scottish history?"

"Mary, Queen of Scots. Not too much."

"Did you see *Braveheart?*"

"No. Too violent."

"A profound movie. Heroic people. How they could prevail against England as long as they did. We'll rent it when we get home. You can close your eyes at the bloodier parts. Just the thought of their strength and determination, their will to survive keeps me going at times. We've got it so easy today because of people like them. Our ancestors, the ancestors everywhere who kept going against all odds."

"I guess I can survive this walk then. You have a deep sense of romance and idealism that you haven't shown me before. I like it. I think you're in touch with your ancestors here." She stopped to look into his eyes and kiss him, then they walked on for about half an hour. Christina had all the freezing ruggedness she could stand, so they headed back to the castle.

It was three days before they heard from Eric. He finally called. He was interested in their project and wanted to discuss it in some depth. John wanted them to meet in their room, but Christina was afraid it was bugged. John did not tell Eric this because he didn't want Eric to be put off by Christina's paranoia so soon and change his mind about working with them. He suggested they meet over dinner in the castle restaurant, and Eric agreed. John reserved one of the more private tables in a corner.

"This is exciting!" Christina said as she was putting on her finest emerald and diamond necklace. "I hardly ever get a chance to wear this jewelry back home."

"Well, don't wear it now, either," John admonished.

"Why the hell not?"

"We don't want him to think you're loaded with money."

"Well, I am."

"The more he thinks you have, the more he'll want to spend. We don't want that. Play a little poker and don't show him your hand."

Oh, all right." She took off her necklace. "I'll have to put it back in the hotel safe before dinner."

Eric was waiting for them at their table. They engaged in some small talk while they had drinks and ordered dinner. Then the conversation turned to the screenplay. Christina became distracted as she looked for suspicious characters among the other diners. "John," she interrupted. "There's that man we saw in the pub the other day."

John looked around. He recognized the man. Eric recognized him, too. "He's one of ours. Don't know exactly what he does, though. Kind of a surly looking guy, but harmless."

Christina relaxed a little. She tried to pay attention to John and Eric's discussion but found the business details boring. By the time dinner was over, they had hammered out the details of the contract which would be then be reviewed by their respective entertainment lawyers.

After dinner and Eric had left, John suggested a walk. "I think it's too cold out, John."

"Wait in the lobby and I'll get our coats."

"Okay." Christina sat on a sofa by the fire while John went upstairs. He returned shortly with the coats. They bundled up and went out. It was a clear night. Christina stopped to look up at the sky. "Look!" she cried.

John sighed. He remembered the nighttime drive to Vegas and his speeding ticket because of her seeing something in the sky. "Are you going to ruin our romantic evening with your imaginings?"

"There really is something!"

He looked up. Yes, there was a large, bright pulsating light above them Then the light seemed to divide into three separate pulsating lights. "Looks like flares or something."

"Something is right, John! Let's get out of here."

His curiosity was aroused. "Let's watch it a minute, see what happens."

Christina wasn't waiting around. She ran back to the safety of the castle.

John took out his cell phone and took a video of the object. After a minute or two the lights merged again, then the light sped across the sky and disappeared.

Trying to figure out what he had just seen, he returned to the castle with some trepidation. How was he going to explain this to Christina to calm her down? He thought she would have gone up to their room, so he went up to look for her, but she wasn't there.

He found her in the hotel lobby sitting on a sofa by the fire. A few other people were there enjoying drinks in the lobby.

He sat down next to Christina and put his arm around her. She was shivering. "You're really upset, aren't you, sweetheart?"

"I can't seem to warm up. See? There really are aliens, and they tracked me here!"

"It's some military experiment, that's all. This area is sparsely populated. A good place to test experimental craft, just like the desert back in California."

"Make us reservations to fly out of here tonight!"

"I don't think we'll be able to get a flight until morning. I'll make us a reservation when we go upstairs. How about a hot toddy or something? It'll warm you up and help you sleep."

Christina couldn't help smiling at that. "Who do you think I am, your grandmother?"

"Just trying to be helpful."

"A hot chocolate might help."

"I doubt if they have that in the bar."

"How about decaf with Bailey's Irish Cream?"

"Okay. Will you be okay for a minute while I go get it?"

"I think so."

He brought her the drink, and one for himself.

"When I get home, I'm going to get a full body scan."

"Why would you do such a silly thing?"

"It's not silly. I think there's some tracking device imbedded in me somewhere. It might not be in my brain, the only part of me they scanned in the sanitarium. Some kind of implants have been found in about ten people in various parts of their bodies. Little pieces of strange metal with some nerve cells around them that don't belong in those parts of the body."

"You've been watching too many shows about aliens, or spending too much time on weird websites."

"Someone has to stop them. I'll be glad when our movie is finished. Maybe then the threat will be taken seriously."

"There are so many sci-fi films and books out there, I'm afraid yours won't be taken any more seriously than the others."

"You've got to make it so they take it seriously!"

John sighed. "Drink up, and let's go to bed."

"After you make reservations for the first plane out of here."

"Right."

Back home in Santa Rosa again, John worked on perfecting the screenplay according to suggestions Eric had scribbled on his manuscript. He agreed with most of the changes, but not all. He wanted to keep a couple of things the way they were.

Christina looked over the requested changes and agreed with them, then she tended to some business—checking up on her trust fund, checking her bill pay account, and moving some money from her money market account to her checking account. She had a reason for making more cash available.

"John, dear, what kind of car would you like to have?"

"I have a perfectly good car now, with room in it for stuff like dog crates and dogs. Why?"

"If you had a second car, what kind would you like?"

He laughed. "That Jag we rented in Scotland was cool."

"Same color?"

"Silver? Sure. Maybe a sportier model, though. Why?"

"Riding to the country club in your lower middle-class SUV is a little embarrassing. People will think we don't belong there."

"Well, I don't."

"Yes, you do. You're an business manager, a screenwriter…"

"A dog walker and your babysitter."

"Come on, we're going to the Jag dealer and get another car. I'm buying. It will be my car if you don't want to claim it, but you'll have to drive it when I want you to."

"Twist my arm."

Christina playfully twisted his arm. "Let's take the dogs."

"They're not fully housebroken—or car broken—yet. One of them peed on the seat when we were bringing them home from the kennel. Put them in their crate."

"Oh, all right."

On the way over to the Jaguar dealer, John asked, "Who's going to drive the new car home, if they have one in stock? You said you never wanted to drive again."

"I was exaggerating. You'll be right behind me. By the way, let's stop at my bank to get a cashier's check."

"But you don't know how much it will be or if they even have one we want in stock."

"I can get a blank one and fill in the amount when we know."

"You can do that?"

"I can do that."

As luck would have it, the dealer had the car John wanted on hand. He got the price down a little for her.

"You drive your car and I'll drive the Jag. I'm going to have to follow you because I'm not sure of the way to go."

"Okay."

"You'll have to keep your eye on the rearview mirror to make sure I'm close behind."

"No problem."

Christina climbed into the Jag and shut the door. The window was down, and John gave her kiss on her forehead. Then he got into his car and started the engine. They headed for home.

While they waited for Eric to be available to start work on the movie, John refined the screenplay some more. Every time he read it, he found more to correct or revise.

He and Christina practiced more songs. He thought they were ready to put on a performance at the country club, and Christina said she would give it a try. They auditioned for the restaurant manager. He liked their act, the sexy Christina in her slinky dress, and John's witty remarks between numbers. He wanted to hire them for the following Friday night. John negotiated a deal for them.

"Are you ready for your debut, Christina?"

"I'm a little nervous."

"Lots of singers get nervous before a performance. Some of them even throw up."

"I'm not nervous about singing."

"Then what's there to be nervous about?"

"Who might be there watching me."

"Who?"

"You know who."

"Oh, THEM. I don't think they'd harm you in front of a crowd."

"There will be lights on us. We won't be able to see the crowd very well. I don't want to do this. Let's just forget it."

"You can't keep living your life in fear like this. It's keeping you from enjoying life and expressing yourself. It's no kind of life. Now put the dogs in their crate and let's go."

She acquiesced, and coaxed the puppies into their crate. "They're getting too big to share a crate. We're going to have to get another one."

They went downstairs to the garage. "Let's take my car," John teased.

"No, we're not!"

"Just kidding."

They arrived in style at the country club. The valet parked the Jag as they went in. John opened the piano and turned on the amp and checked the mics. He set one binder of music on the music stand for Christina and put one on the piano for himself. Christina thumbed through her music while he went and got them a couple of glasses of wine and had the bartender turn off the canned music.

Christina looked over the guests, seemed to relax a little when she didn't see anyone unusual. "Good evening, ladies and gentlemen," she began. "I hope you enjoy our music tonight. I'm Christina and this is John Davis at the piano." The audience applauded. Then she sat down at the table provided for them while John played a couple of tunes. After that she sang a few numbers, then he soloed again, and so it went. The evening was a success. The audience loved them.

After they were finished, Christina was sipping her wine while John closed up the piano. A woman came over and sat down with Christina.

"You're very good," the woman said. "I understand you're making a movie about aliens taking over the world. Tell me about it."

"What? How did you get in here? John! Come here!"

John came over. "What is it?"

"This woman says we're making a movie." Christina got up from the table and grabbed her purse. "We're leaving, and don't bother me again," she said angrily to the woman.

On their way out they ran into Bob Alexander. "Can I buy you a drink?" Bob asked.

John looked at Christina. She shrugged her shoulders. "Okay," John replied. They sat down with Bob.

"That woman a friend of yours?" he asked Christina.

"I never saw her before," Christina said.

"Funny. She said she was a friend of yours. She was asking about you. She wanted to know how your movie was going."

"What? How would she know about that?"

"I told her I didn't know anything about a movie. How is it going, by the way? Are you going to use Eliot?"

"I don't think so," John replied. "Christina has decided on someone else. Someone we met through a newspaper colleague. Did that woman tell you who she was?"

"No. I introduced myself, but then she went to the ladies' room. I didn't see her again until I saw her talking to you. I doubt if she's a member. I wonder how she got in here."

They engaged in some small talk while they finished their drinks, then left with Bob suggesting a game of golf soon.

—ᴧᴧ—

A couple of days later John and Christina went grocery shopping. They were standing in the checkout line when Christina saw a copy of the tabloid *Exposed* on the rack next to her. She pulled out a copy and stared at the cover. "John," she said softly.

He turned to her. "What is it, my love?"

"She took our picture." She handed the paper to him.

He read the headline aloud. "Bad Boy John Davis Plays Second Fiddle to Multi-Millionaire Singer Christina Markham."

"What a bitch!" Christina said.

"Oh, I don't know. This might be good publicity." He smiled a sort of self-satisfied smile. "I've never been known as a bad boy before. I could get to like it. Seriously, people want to see a movie made by people of some notoriety." He picked up several papers and put them with the groceries.

"I don't want people to know where I am or what I'm doing."

"You don't care if people know. Just aliens."

"Oh, yeah. I forgot—not."

In the car, Christina read the article aloud. "'John Davis, you may recall, wrote that hilariously stupid "Second Coming" article in the *Bay View* based on a story by Larkspur heiress Christina Markham and was dismissed from the paper. Since he couldn't get another reporting job, he went to work for Markham as an accompanist. They were recently seen gigging at the exclusive Vista Heights Country Club lounge. Rumor has it they are living together in an ostentatious mansion in Vista Heights and are preparing to produce a film about an extraterrestrial invasion. Sounds like a copycat Independence Day or Cowboys and Aliens. Can't you come up with your own ideas, Davis?'

"This is absurd, John! How can she do this?"

John laughed. "I love it! Don't you see what good publicity this is for us? I can't wait to get going on this film."

"People are not going the take the film seriously, she's made so light of it."

"So what? People aren't going to remember exactly what she said, but they'll remember they read something about the movie. If nothing else, they'll want to see just how bad it is. If you want people to take the theme seriously, you can talk about it on talk shows. We'll get some offers when the film's out."

"I don't want to go on national television."

"If you want to people to hear your message, you gotta do it."

Christina sighed. "This is getting complicated."

"Don't worry about the future. When it gets here, we just go on TV and talk. Oh, wait. It's the aliens again. They might see you on TV and know where you are even if the show is taped ahead of time and you are back home when it's aired."

"Stop making fun of me."

"What we really need to worry about is training the dogs. They can't even shake hands. They're chewing up my shoes and emptying the wastebaskets and generally running wild."

Christina laughed. "Yeah. They're pretty funny."

"Chewed up shoes are not funny, Christina. Let's take the dogs to obedience school."

"Yes, dear."

And I have to get some new shoes."

"Sorry about your shoes."

"Me, too."

The obedience training went well at the training facility, but not so well at home. They went to several sessions so the humans could practice being firm and consistent. Some headway was made. John learned to keep his closet door closed and Christina learned to keep the bathroom door closed so the puppies couldn't unroll the toilet paper and chew on the bathroom rugs. They learned not to leave the puppies unattended in the living room with the expensive hand woven Persian rugs so that they could no longer chew on the fringes. They also learned to crate the puppies when they wanted to go for a swim without them.

Now that the dog difficulties were diminished Christina decided she wanted a couple of kittens.

"NO!" John said. "We've just reclaimed our home from the dogs and now you want to release a couple of crazy cats to swing on the drapes and climb the screens? Sharpen their claws on the sofas and pounce on us from the top of the refrigerator? We're going to be too busy with the movie to mess with them."

"All right," she said. "We'll wait until the movie is finished."

It was mid-July when Eric finally showed up. He would stay in the pool house. He had a full-time assistant, Merilee Weathers, who would stay in the caretaker's apartment.

Christina felt comfortable with Eric and Merilee and was glad more people were staying on the property. Also, it would be nice to have another woman around.

"The first order of business," John announced after they arrived, "is to barbecue a chicken, that is if you aren't vegetarians."

"No, we're not," Eric said.

"I tried it," Merilee said, "but I felt I couldn't get enough nutrition. I was tired all the time, and my brain didn't seem to work very well. I try to stick with chicken and fish, though. Tomorrow I'll get some groceries to stock the apartment and the pool house with so you don't have to feed us all the time."

Eric explained how they would start working. "During the next couple of days we're going to read through the screenplay and make out a list of tentative expenses. We need an advance of $10,000.00 for our time to get things down on paper. I should have a working contract drawn up in about a week. In the meantime you should come up with a name for your film company and open an operating trust account. When I give you the budget, you'll deposit that amount in the account so I know the money will be there as needed. I'll have to see an official statement of how much is in the account. Do you have enough money to fund this project yourselves or are we going to have to go looking for it?"

"We have enough," Christina replied. "I'm not sure we would want someone else involved financially, but it's not out of the question." She got her checkbook and wrote out a check for the advance to Eric.

After dinner Eric and Merilee retired to their respective abodes. John and Christina tried to come up with a company name. "How about 'Saving the Planet'? Christina suggested.

"That's probably being used by some global warming group. I think the company name should be more generic, not tied to a specific film. What if we want to do another film someday? Let's see, uh, how about 'Markham-Davis Productions'?"

"Boring and forgettable," Christina said. "How about 'Perfect Productions?'

"Let's not waste any more time on this, Christina. Just go with 'Markham-Davis,' 'Markham-Davis Films.'"

"I don't know. Maybe it should just be 'Markham Films.' Are you thinking this is a partnership?"

"I'm thinking that so far I've done most of the work, and I will most likely be doing most of the work from now on."

"Well, it's my story and my money. I'm taking all the risk while you're getting paid every month. Are you expecting half the profits, assuming there will be any?"

"I'm not getting paid to be the executive producer, which in effect is what I will be. You can pay me a million up front, or you can give me a decent share of the revenue."

"And what percentage would that be, do you think?"

"Thirty percent."

"I'm thinking twenty-five."

"You're a hard bargainer, my dear. Okay, it's a deal." John stretched out his hand and Christina shook it. "We'll need an entertainment lawyer to draw up a contract," he said.

"Don't you trust me?"

"Not that far. We'll need one anyway to go over the contract with Eric and any other contracts that will have to be negotiated with actors, musicians, and so forth."

"It's getting to sound very complicated. I'd better give you thirty per cent. Let's shake on that," Christina said.

—⁓—

John contacted an entertainment lawyer in Santa Monica because he thought a lawyer experienced in the film industry would be best. He checked out the lawyer's references and found him to be highly regarded. He talked to the lawyer on the phone and then sent him a retainer so there wouldn't be a delay in getting legal advice on the contract. When Eric and Merilee brought over the contract, he scanned it and e-mailed it to the lawyer.

That evening John barbecued chicken and the four of them had a sumptuous feast under the stars. After dinner Merilee asked if they could turn off the lights to look at the moon and the stars. Christina turned off the patio lights. "It's lovely," Merilee said. "You have a magical place here, more beautiful than most places I've worked."

"Yeah," John agreed, "but it's pretty isolated. Far to go if we want to see people or go shopping."

"I don't mind that," Christina said. "I like being away from people most of the time."

Merilee was looking up at the stars. "There's a plane or something." She pointed to it. They all looked up.

Right away John said, "Yeah, just a plane."

The pulsating light got brighter and brighter as it got closer.

"That's the UFO we saw in Scotland!" Christina exclaimed. She jumped out of her chair and scrambled into the kitchen. "You'd better come in, too, before they get you!"

The others wouldn't go in. They stayed out on the patio and watched. The UFO appeared to be about thirty feet across. It hovered silently overhead for a couple of minutes, then moved slowly over the orchard and seemed to land on the other side. They couldn't be sure because their view was cut off by the trees and a dip in the landscape on the other side.

"What IS that thing?" Merilee asked.

"I don't know," John replied.

"Wanna check it out?" Eric suggested.

"Okay, but I don't want to leave Christina alone. She really freaked at the one we saw in Scotland. Merilee, could you go in and stay with her?"

"Gladly. I don't want to get too close to that thing." She headed for the kitchen door, then turned back to them. "Have you got a gun?"

"I guess it would be a good idea." John headed for the kitchen. The door was locked, the house was dark. "Christina! Open the door!" He pounded on the wood frame anxiously. Christina peered out at him, then unlocked it.

"The power's out, John. Can you turn it back on?"

"I'll see." Merilee went in and John went to the electrical box on the side of the house near the garage. All the circuits had kicked off. He shook his head in disbelief, then flipped them back on. The outside lights came on. He went back to the kitchen where Christina had turned on every light possible.

"Christina, get me a gun." Christina hurried away and came back with a rifle and some ammo.

"I don't think we should wave rifles around. It might attract unnecessary fire. Just a revolver—two revolvers. And a flashlight," he added. She scurried away again and returned with two revolvers, a box of bullets, and her derringer.

"For me," she said of the derringer.

"Merilee is staying in the house with you. Eric and I will check it out. Don't worry. It might just be a hot-air balloon."

"In the dark?" she responded in a shrill, nervous voice. "I don't think so."

John went out with the guns and a couple of flashlights. "Call 911, Merilee. Tell them what's going on. Even if it's not dangerous, it's still trespassing."

"Okay, John."

Eric and John loaded their guns. "I don't know if these guns are registered, Eric, so if the sheriff shows up, be discreet."

"Gotcha," Eric replied.

"And keep the flashlight pointed at the ground so it will be less noticeable." With that, they headed off toward the orchard.

"There's a path through here," John said pointing his flashlight on to the path. He led the way, and Eric followed.

Eric chuckled. "This is the first time I ever got to live the film I was going to produce."

"Well, I hope it doesn't get too gory. I have no idea what we're going to find." He lowered his voice to almost a whisper. "We're getting close. We'd better be quiet."

They reached the edge of the orchard and had to walk a little ways in the open before they could see over the ridge. They shut off their flashlights and peered down the hill. The light of the half moon washed dimly over a large silvery round object. No light was coming from it. It sat there silently. No signs of life, people or otherwise.

"Should we go down there?" Eric asked.

"I don't know. Maybe wait a minute. See if something happens." They waited several minutes, but nothing happened. "Let's get closer, but not too close. I've heard some of these things put out radiation." They started down the hill carefully, because it was hard to see where to step without their flashlights. Suddenly Eric let out a yell as he stumbled over a rock and went rolling down several feet.

A blinding searchlight came on at the spacecraft, the light reaching out to sweep the area. John hit the ground and flattened himself in the tall dry grass. Eric did the same. "Sorry," he whispered. They pulled their guns out of their pockets and held them ready.

"Maybe it's a drone and there's no one in it," John whispered. "I saw a news photo of one that looked like that, on the back of a truck, but it was smaller."

"I don't want to go down there and find out what it is," Eric said.

The light swept the area a few times and then shut off. They had to wait a few minutes for their night vision to return before they could see much of anything again. The craft was still sitting there silently. Eric took out his cell phone to take a picture of it. "Damn. My cell phone is totally dead."

"Magnetic field. These things are said to cause electrical disturbances. That reminds me. I took a video of the one we saw in Scotland." John heard a siren in the distance. The sound was getting closer. "Must be the sheriff."

"Took them long enough," Eric said. "We could be dead by now."

Suddenly the craft was humming. It became enveloped in an eerie glow. It rose up into the sky and seemed to vanish in an instant. "Let's go down and see if it left any marks on the ground."

"It's too dark out here. What if the area is full of radiation? Let's wait until morning, or until the sheriff gets here."

"He won't have seen it. He probably won't believe us. Somebody must have been inside it to hear the siren, to take off like that."

John shrugged his shoulders and started back up the hill. They were still clutching their guns when they opened the gate. John remembered at the last second before a deputy spotted him and stuffed it in his pocket. Eric did likewise. Christina and Merilee were outside on the patio with two deputies. They had already told the deputies what they had seen.

"Did you guys see anything else?"

"Yeah," John replied. "It landed on the other side of the orchard, down a small hill. It was just sitting there, dark and silent. Then Eric tripped over a rock and rolled down the hill a few feet and let out a yell. A searchlight came on, but we stayed down so I don't think they saw us. Then we heard your siren and they took off, vanished into the sky. The ship glowed and hummed as it took off."

"That's it," Eric said. "The diameter was about thirty feet."

"We'll file a report," one of the deputies said. "That's about all we can do now it's gone."

John was surprised they didn't want to take a look. "What about checking for evidence, marks on the ground and whatever."

"It's too dark to see anything now. We'll send someone over in the morning to take a look." He looked at the table with wine glasses and a couple of bottles. "You guys been drinking or something?"

"We're not drunk! We know what we saw!" Christina protested. "Don't you believe we saw something? They're after me!"

"Sure, sure. We'll be in touch. We gotta go now." The deputies turned and walked into the house, followed by the incredulous witnesses, and left by the front door.

"I can see we're well protected by local law enforcement," Eric said. "Say, John, I'd like to see that video you told me about."

"What video?" Christina asked.

"Oh, nothing," John said.

Eric didn't get that John didn't want her to know about it. "The one you took of that UFO you saw in Scotland."

"Oh, that. It wasn't much of anything."

"I want to see it," Christina said.

"Me, too," chimed in Merilee.

"All right. I forgot all about it. I'll send it to my computer and we can take a look."

He turned on his laptop and then his cell phone. He couldn't find the video. He couldn't find anything. Everything stored on his cell phone had been wiped out. "Shit! Everything's gone! Check yours, Eric."

Eric turned on his phone. "Yep. Wiped clean. We got too close."

"You should have told me about the video," Christina admonished. "You would have downloaded it before, and now we'd have it."

"I didn't want to upset you."

"I would have been much less upset than I am now! Let's contact someone who cares, some UFO investigators. Those deputies won't be back. They don't believe us."

"Yeah," Eric said. "Maybe they can find some evidence left at the landing site."

"I'll call someone," John said, "but, Christina, don't spill your life story to them. That's for the movie."

"I'm not as stupid as you think, Mister Know-it-all. What I know is we might get some publicity out of this."

"Yeah," John said. "It might be in the sheriff's log and get into the newspaper with our address, then we'll have a bunch of rubberneckers stomping all over our property and peering in our windows." Christina raised her eyebrows and gave him a look he had some difficulty deciphering. "Oh, excuse me, I mean YOUR property, madam."

"I'm an unmarried woman, so it's 'miss' or 'mademoiselle.' Some editor you are, ha, ha." Christina loved it when she could catch him in a mistake, no matter how miniscule.

John scowled and got on the Internet to find a UFO investigator. He got a phone number and made the call. A real person answered the phone. They would come out early in the morning with their equipment to run some tests on the site and interview everyone.

—⁓—

As soon as the sun was up, the investigative crew arrived. John and the others went down to the site with them. Most of the crew set up their equipment while one crew member questioned the witnesses at length. When it was Christina's turn to be interviewed, she told them about seeing the same craft in Scotland. "I've been abducted a couple of times. I think they're following me. They were following us on our way to Vegas, too. Do you have any idea why they're doing that?"

"No, I don't. Some people say they've been abducted many times. If it's any comfort, nobody that we know of has been killed by extraterrestrials."

"Well, it is actually a relief to hear that. What about implanted tracking devices? I think there's one in me somewhere."

"I don't know. Some people think they have one, but evidence has been elusive. Just call us if you get another visitation. See if you can get a photo or video."

"I'll try. Do you know someone who can give me a body scan to see if there's a tracking device imbedded in me?"

He wrote down a name and number for her. "This doctor has tested a few people. If anyone can find something, he can."

The crew took photographs, measured the imprints, took soil and plant samples, and went over the area with a Geiger counter. "There's an unusually high level of radiation around here," Jordan

Anders, the chief investigator, told them. "That's often the case with these landings. Some scorched earth, also usual." He pointed to the three depressions in the soil. "Some kind of landing gear, to be expected with a landing. Some of these signs can be faked by hoaxers, but it's not so easy to fake the high level of radiation. We still have to test the soil and plant samples to be sure, but I think you've got a real live UFO landing."

"Could you leave our address out of your report?" John asked. "We don't want people traipsing around out here."

"No problem. Your address will be confidential."

The UFO investigators gathered up their equipment and left. Merilee and Eric returned to their respective quarters. John and Christina went inside and Christina locked the door behind them. "John, make sure all the doors and windows are locked, and lock the doggie door, too."

"The doggie door? It's broad daylight. I don't think anyone's going to be crawling through the doggie door in the daytime. How will the dogs get out?"

"You'll take them out when they need to go. I'm staying in the house."

John did her bidding and locked up the house. "It feels claustrophobic, being shut in like this in the middle of the day." This was one of the many times John questioned his own sanity to be living with her, to have anything at all to do with her.

Christina activated the burglar alarm. "See," she said, "it's just like I told you. I'm being followed by aliens, and they know where I live."

"Perhaps you are being followed, but we still don't know whether they're aliens or humans."

"They keep finding me. There must be some tracking device in me. I'm going to get a body scan and find out. I got the name of a doctor who researches these things. If he finds something he can remove it."

John had his doubts about it, but he didn't voice them. He knew there wasn't much use in trying to deter Christina once she made up her mind.

"We need to go over the contract if you want to get your movie made. Let's sit down at the table and start on it now." Christina sat down with them and studied the details of the contract.

"I want to choose the leading man and woman," she said. "We could play these parts ourselves."

"We need stars, Christina, box-office draws, experienced actors."

"I was joking. I didn't really think it would go over. But I think we should have a voice in who plays our parts."

"Leave it to the experts. They're hiring a casting service. That way we won't have hundreds of people coming out here for auditions."

"About this property rental for some of the scenes. They can use my house in Larkspur. I'm glad I kept it. That will save some money."

"Make a note for Eric."

Christina looked at the budget. "This movie is going to dig deep into my pocket. Look at the cost of just feeding and housing people on location! I think we can do better than that."

"It's a budget. It doesn't mean we have to spend it all."

"Once you have a budget, it's easy to go over it, too."

"I'll find a caterer myself. We don't have to feed them quite so well. Most of the people can eat ordinary food."

"Make a note of everything you think we can save money on, Christina. What about these RVs for the stars? There's a whole wing of the house we don't use. Maybe they could stay there, or Eric and Merilee could."

"Make a note."

"I've got an extensive wardrobe. They could use some of my things."

"Mine, too," John said.

"You're kidding, of course."

"No. I don't know how you'll feel about this, but I rescued some of your father's suits and ties. I wear the same size."

"You did that without my permission?"

"I thought later on you might not be so sensitive."

"I guess it's okay. Maybe they can make use of some of it. I didn't see my father that often in a suit, so I probably wouldn't have even known they were his."

Christina wrote down a final total budget amount she wanted to see, and some of her suggestions. Then they handed the papers over to Merilee. Merilee broke into a smile as she looked over the suggestions. "We know you're financing this film, and we've cut as many corners as we thought we could, but I see a couple of things that will be helpful, like using your house in Larkspur for filming, and also part of your house and property here. I'll discuss it with Eric. You're not going to save much on handling the caterers, and it can be a real headache."

"I'll take your word for it. I don't need any extra headaches."

"Oh, I almost forgot. Property insurance is part of the package, but you should notify your insurance company about what's going on. The people we work with are fairly trustworthy, but you never know, plus some damage may occur, and you may want your insurance company to handle details."

"We'll take care of it."

Contract matters were quickly hashed out and everything agreed upon, so they signed, and work could begin on the film. An experienced screenwriter was hired to go over the play. He worked with John to beef up some of the scenes that he thought needed more action. In most cases John agreed, and they only got into a couple of arguments. All in all, the results were favorable.

Christina was anxious for filming to commence, but it seemed to take forever for actors and crew to be hired. A shooting script had to be completed by the director, and so on and so on.

RVs were brought in for housing, wardrobe, etc. Temporary fencing was installed around the newly formed compound. Eric and Merilee moved into the unused wing of the house and left the pool house and apartment for the leading man and woman. The stars were to be housed in suites at an unnamed hotel in Santa Rosa and would only use the pool house and apartment for preparation and for breaks.

Eric suggested a cocktail party and buffet for the cast and some of the crew a couple of evenings before shooting would begin. It was included in the catering budget, so John and Christina had little to do but look elegant and play the charming host and hostess.

—ᵚᵚ—

The morning of the party, Christina awoke before the sun was up. She was too excited to sleep. She leaned over John and shook him gently. "Wake up, John, dear. It's time to get up. We have a lot to do." He wasn't opening his eyes, so she kissed him on the mouth and he quickly responded, more than she intended.

"Mmm..." he said. "More."

Christina grabbed a roll of breath mints out of the bedside drawer. "Only if we have one of these—morning breath," she said and slipped one into his mouth and one into hers. She kissed him again. "That's better," she said, and they were able to make love before the puppies woke up and started yapping to get out of their crate.

"I wish we could wake up every morning before dawn while the puppies are still asleep," John said as he put on his t-shirt. "It's the only way to get any privacy around here."

"I understand the film crew starts at the break of dawn every morning, so I think you'll be getting your wish whether you like it or not."

They took the dogs out, then had some scrambled eggs and whole wheat toast for breakfast. By the time they finished, the RVs were rolling in. John went out to make sure Eric was directing them to a suitable area.

The cleaning crew arrived to clean the house, the apartment, and the pool house. Christina hovered over them to make sure everything was just so. Fresh flowers were delivered for the pool house and the apartment as well as the main house. The gardeners came to freshen up the grounds. So many people were around whom Christina knew that she felt safe enough to stay home while John took the puppies to Doggie Daycare. They didn't want them underfoot and causing havoc at the party, no matter how cute they were.

Later in the day the caterers came. They took over the kitchen, the dining room, the living room and the patio area to prepare for the party.

Christina went upstairs to rest awhile before getting dressed. John was helping Eric organize his office in the house.

Eric rummaged through one of his boxes and pulled out a thick binder. "Here's a copy of the finished script. Look it over and see what you think. I expect you to be involved in the production, and speak up if you're not satisfied with the dialogue."

John took the binder. "Thanks. I'll do that." He left Eric and went upstairs to the bedroom. Christina was holding up a dress to her and looking in the full-length mirror.

"Is this a formal event?" she asked.

"I don't know."

"Could you ask Eric, please? I need to know what to wear."

"Certainly, my dear." He headed back downstairs and returned shortly with the answer. "Not formal."

"Hmm," she mused and returned the dress to the walk-in closet. John followed her. "I don't know what to wear."

"Maybe you have too many choices."

"Oh, I don't know. Everything's a year or two old. I'm not going to look up to date in anything."

"That's ridiculous." He pulled out some skinny black mid-calf pants and an iridescent lilac-colored, low-cut flimsy blouse. "How about these?"

She twirled a lock of her hair around her finger, thought about it a moment. "I'd need a black tank top underneath." He found one hanging nearby, low-cut and form fitting. "What kind of necklace would I wear with that?"

He shrugged. "Diamonds?"

"Exactly." She opened a drawer and pulled out a thin sculpted necklace made entirely of little diamonds set in white gold.

"Very nice," he said, "but what I want to know is why you keep valuable jewelry loose like that in an unlocked drawer."

"Because I have nowhere else to put it."

"Well, you talked me out of having someone come out and build in a safe for you."

"Maybe I was wrong. Let's have someone come out and put one in. I would set the combination. He wouldn't know what it is. "

"Do you have a key for the bedroom door?"

"Yes, I do. It's here in my jewelry drawer."

"Give it to me. I want to lock the room when we leave, so party people don't wander in and start looking around."

Christina gave him the key. "Now let's pick out what you're going to wear."

John opted for white trousers and a light blue and white print silk shirt that complemented his blue eyes. Christina lamented the fact that she hadn't thought to give him some of her father's diamond rings and a Rolex.

"I don't usually wear jewelry, but I wouldn't turn down a Rolex or two."

"Would you wear a wedding ring if you were married?"

"I don't know. It would probably depend on how much my bride twisted my arm."

"She would twist it a lot," Christina teased while taking hold of his arm and twisting it a little.

John smiled and gently broke away from her grip. "Let's change the subject and get ready for the party."

After dressing they went downstairs. They meandered hand in hand through the rooms and out onto the patio. "What a lavish spread!" Christina said of the *hors d'oeuvres,* "and the decorating is sublime."

"And it's costing you a pretty penny, my sweet."

"Yes, but I wanted to give a party when we moved here, and you wondered who would come. Now we're going to have a houseful of interesting people, and we didn't even have to send out invitations. I hope someone is checking the people who come in."

"What do you mean?"

"You know. Making sure no unsavory people or aliens sneak in."

"Eric said it was only the cast and some of the crew. I'm sure they'll be checking."

"Well, is someone checking the door, or down at the gate?"

"Probably."

"Please find out, John. I don't want any frightening surprises."

"I'm not going to check, Christina," he said, his voice a little elevated in frustration. "You think they're not going to have heavy security with film stars coming here?" John looked out on the patio and yard. "Look there. See those two guys standing there in security uniforms?"

"Oh," she said, and turned and went in the kitchen.

John followed her. "I think it's time we stationed ourselves near the front door to welcome the guests."

They got a couple of glasses of champagne and stood and near the door. The jazz combo had finished setting up, and "Summertime" played softly in the background. Christina clasped John's arm. "Oh, John. This is so exciting. We're going to meet Colin Stewart and Julia Harrington!"

Eric and Merilee joined them. They didn't have to wait long before people started trickling in. Supporting actors and actresses, bit players, camera men, a hair dresser, a couple of makeup artists, a set designer and his assistant, film editors, the music supervisor, and so on. After a while, The trickle stopped. Everyone but the stars seemed to be there.

"Where's Colin and Julia?" Christina wanted to know.

"Oh, they always show up late, if at all," Eric answered.

"You mean they might not even come?"

"It's possible they won't. Why don't you go mingle with the other guests? If I see them, I'll bring them over and introduce you."

John and Christina refilled their champagne glasses, nibbled on some *hors d'oeuvres,* and mingled. Well, John did most of the actual mingling. He chatted amiably with the guests. Christina stood next to him and said little, unless asked a question. She spent most of her time looking around for suspicious-looking persons. Finally, she found one. She tugged on John's sleeve.

"What is it, my sweet?"

She pulled on his sleeve and moved him away from the people he was talking to. She pointed. "Over there. That's the strange man we saw in the cafe in Scotland."

"Oh, him. Eric said he was with their company. Harmless. Why don't you try to relax and enjoy yourself? No one's going to hurt you."

"That's easy for you to say."

"Let's get some food." He herded her toward the buffet table. There they saw Julia Harris and Colin Stewart filling up their plates. Suddenly Christina was no longer shy. She grabbed a plate and approached Julia Harris. "Oh, you're Julia, aren't you? I'm Christina Markham, producer and co-writer of the film."

Julia smiled and nodded. "Glad to meet you. It's quite a script you wrote. I'm going to enjoy working on the film."

"I can't take all the credit. John Davis here put together most of my ideas very well."

John shook hands with Julia, then Colin. "Glad to meet you."

"Likewise," Colin said.

"A lovely party, Christina."

"Thanks. There again, most of the credit goes to someone else—Eric Dawson."

The chitchat went on for a few minutes more, then Julia and Colin excused themselves. "Must mingle," Colin quipped, and they quickly disappeared.

"I don't see where they went," Christina remarked.

"My guess is they're not mingling, but found some secluded nook where they can eat in peace."

John looked up at the balcony where the jazz combo was playing. "I'm going to talk to the musicians about you singing a song or two, if you don't mind."

"I don't mind at all. It would be fun."

Christina followed John upstairs and they performed a couple of numbers with the drummer and bass player while the pianist and sax player took a break and went for food. People stopped talking when Christina started singing. Afterwards they applauded. Julia appeared out of nowhere to compliment her. "You know, or maybe you don't, that I'm not much of a singer. This film calls for singing and I want you to sing behind me. I'll lip sync in the film after you've recorded it. What do you think?"

"I'd be honored, Julia. I just hope I can do it well enough."

"Oh, I'm sure you can. Just tell Eric and he'll arrange it. Okay?"

"Okay!"

"John! Julia wants me sing for the movie. We'll have to practice a lot."

"Does she want me to be the pianist?"

"I don't know. She didn't say, but I'd rather sing with you than some stranger. Would you mind?"

"Hey, when do I get another chance to be in a movie?"

"Yeah, you might actually be on screen, and I won't get to be. I'd be jealous."

He smiled. "I can live with that. Can you?"

"I'll ask Eric. You're certainly handsome enough to be in a movie. Maybe I can be a guest at the party in the film."

"Thank you, my love. I'll be indebted to you forever." He kissed her hand.

Someone shouted, "Look! A UFO!" People started pouring out the patio doors and looking up to the sky.

"John! It's back!" Christina ran down the stairs, John chasing after her. A cameraman who had been taking a digital video of the party started filming the commotion as people poured out the doors and looked up. Then he went out and filmed them from the front as they looked up and then he started filming the UFO outside. John pushed his way through the bunched up people to get to the cameraman.

He said to him, "The UFO will erase your images. It happened to me. You'd better turn that off and get it out of here now. Let me put it down in the wine cellar. Lots of rock. It might shield it."

"Is it real, do you think? I think it's a stunt by Special Effects or the prop people."

"Is it?" John asked.

"Well, I don't know, but they often do crazy things at parties."

"Unless you're sure, let me put that camera downstairs. Better what you have already than nothing. This UFO has been here before."

"Really? Then I guess I'd better let you hide it away." He turned off his camera and handed it over to John. "I've got a little Canon with nothing on it I can try." The cameraman took out his Canon camera as John turned away and took the stairs two at a time down to the wine cellar.

The strange man from the pub in Scotland that Christina was afraid of approached her. "Pretty good stunt," he said.

"Stunt? That's no stunt. That's a real extraterrestrial spaceship."

He laughed a scurrilous laugh. "We'll see, won't we?"

"I saw you in Scotland. Who are you?"

"Oh, just one of the crew."

"What do you do?" she demanded.

He looked away. "Someone's calling me," he said and abruptly turned and walked away.

Christina looked around frantically for John. She didn't find him but she did find Eric. "Eric. Is this one of your company's stunts?"

Eric looked at her thoughtfully. "A stunt? Hmm. Nobody said anything about it, but they don't usually tell me if they're doing something crazy, especially something this disturbing." He shook his head. "Possible, but I kinda doubt it."

"What about the time we saw it before? Could that also be a stunt?"

"The same likelihood. Less likely, actually. The cell phones were wiped out and the electricity went out. I don't know how they would have done that."

At that moment the UFO rose into the air and disappeared.

"There. It's gone. Better, Christina?"

"A little, but it's still very creepy. And speaking of creepy, that weird guy from Scotland is here. He was acting creepy, too."

"How so?"

"Oh, I can't explain it. Have you seen John?"

"Not for a while."

Christina continued her search for John. She still couldn't find him. She gave up and sat down on a sofa and wrung her hands.

Meanwhile the people started coming back inside. John had come up from the wine cellar, only to go back down to retrieve the camera when the UFO had gone. On his way back to the cameraman he saw Christina in the living room. He took her hand. "Come on, Baby Cakes, it's gone. Let's get this camera back to its owner."

She went willingly, clasping his hand tightly. They found the cameraman watching footage on his Canon.

"So it didn't get wiped out, eh?"

"No," the man said. "I got some good footage. Not as good as my movie camera, but it'll do."

John handed him the camera. The cameraman turned it on and looked in the viewer. "Hey, still works. This will be good."

"Great," John said. Christina tugged at his sleeve. "See you later."

"John! Eric doesn't think it's a stunt."

"Look, there was no problem with electronics or the lights this time. More than likely, it was a stunt. What exactly did he say?"

"Well, he thought unlikely. Possible, but unlikely."

"There you go. It's possibly a stunt. We'll probably hear about it soon. The guys who did it will probably want to brag about it."

But nobody took credit for it or bragged about it that night. No one seemed to know anything about it. The party broke up early because people were unsettled, nervous. There was a lot of food left over. The caterers wrapped it up and refrigerated it. Eric said they could serve it on the first day of shooting instead of calling in the caterers for that day.

Christina had a great deal of trouble sleeping that night. She woke John up at two in the morning because she was hungry. They hadn't gotten a chance to eat much the night before, so they headed down to the kitchen where they had some *hors d'oeuvres*. John made her drink a glass of tawny port to help her sleep. It worked.

After the excitement of anticipating the party and having it, the next day was kind of a letdown for John and Christina. Film people were running around getting things ready for the shoot the following day. John went to pick up the dogs at Doggie Daycare.

Christina busied herself looking out the windows for spacecraft and straightening up the house. Although the caterers had left everything clean, they hadn't returned things to their proper places. Christina liked to have all the furniture and knickknacks in certain places. She didn't like things moved around, unless it was her idea. Once John had rearranged the furniture while Christina was upstairs. When she came down, she had what John called "a hissy fit" until he put everything back the way it had been.

"Why does everything have to be just so? Don't you like change?"

I don't like getting up in the middle of the night when I hear a strange noise and tripping over furniture in the dark that is not where it's supposed to be."

"Why don't you just turn on a light?"

"Get a brain, John! I don't want the entities making the noise to see me. Not only that, you don't have any sense of proportion or style when it comes to decorating."

"Sure I do," he said with a laugh.

"Not so anyone else can recognize it, so just leave it to me."

Thereafter, he didn't touch anything without her permission.

Soon the puppies were home again and dashing in to greet Christina, rearranging the area rugs and knocking over a floor lamp and breaking its antique shade. John wondered why she didn't scold the puppies the way she did him. All she did was get down on one knee and welcome the puppies as they licked her face.

"Where's my kiss?" John wanted to know. Christina got up off the floor and gave him one.

"While there are so many people around, you should feel comfortable enough that I can go out for a short run. I'm getting out of shape living this life of luxury,"

"No problem. Better yet, why don't the dogs and I come with you? We could use the exercise, too."

John winced. "They don't run fast enough yet, and they don't run where I want them to, or when I want them to. The idea is that I get some exercise."

"Oh, all right. I'll just stay home and bake cookies or something like a good housewife."

"Tomorrow we'll go for a walk with the dogs."

He kissed her and went out for his run.

Christina and John were allowed to watch when filming first began. Christina soon made a nuisance of herself trying to tell the director what to do. After they got into an argument, she was banished from the area. John was allowed to stay, but Christina wouldn't hear of it. "Let's go for that walk you promised. You can come back later."

Reluctantly, he did her bidding, thinking it would keep her from further argument with the director. They didn't bother to get the dogs, just started walking about the property.

"I can't believe that director treated me that way! Who does he think he is?"

"Uh, the director?"

"Doesn't he realize I'm paying his salary?"

"I think he knows that, but a good director is not a yes man… or a yes woman."

"Well, I'm not one, either."

"I know. How well I know. Look, Christina, we're all going to be reviewing the scenes after they're shot—you, me, Eric, Merilee. That's the time to give our input. In the meantime, let the director do his job and try not to disrupt the shooting, okay?"

"On the way out, I saw him using my idea."

"Maybe he already had the same idea. Leave him alone."

They walked the entire perimeter of the property, and passed through the UFO landing area on their way back to the house. Christina stopped. "Oh my God, John! Look!"

John looked around. "What? I don't see anything,"

"That's just it. Somebody went to a great deal of trouble to erase all the marks of the landing, and covered the area with grass clippings and other stuff."

"Probably the gardeners thought the bare ground was a good place to dump the grass cuttings. It'll replenish the soil."

"Maybe they're connected with the so-called gardener at my other house."

He laughed again, "Whatever. We can't undo it now."

"Maybe we should move to another country. Just get on a plane and go before they can follow us,"

"If you think they can't follow us—whoever you think is following us, think again. Remember the UFO in Scotland?"

"How can I forget? Or the one on the way to Vegas? And don't try to tell me I'm imagining everything."

"I wouldn't dare. Only some things."

"We have to stop them somehow. I can't take much more of this."

"Let's go in," John said, "We should have some lunch."

"Sometimes I think food is all you think about."

"No. There's one other thing I think about, more than food."

He stopped and embraced her. She pushed him away.

"Not now. You're just trying to make me stop thinking,"

"Why do you want to keep thinking about it?"

"I have to think of a way to prevent the aliens from taking over."

John shook his head and walked to the house, held the door open for her.

—◦◦◦—

Filming on location at their house was soon finished and the film crew started filming at the Larkspur house. Living space was too limited there so the film crew continued to live at the Santa Rosa location until it was time to go on location in Scotland. They were able to get a good rate for filming in and around the castle where John and Christina had stayed. Christina wanted to go there, but Eric said it was a waste of her time because she wouldn't be allowed on the set.

Christina waited impatiently, and John, too, although less impatiently, for several months for the film to be finished, She called Eric so often for progress reports that he finally asked her not to call again. He was very busy, he said, and she should just wait for him to call her when it was done. Finally, after several months she got the call.

Eric flew in from L.A. with a DVD copy of the film for their review. "It's good, Christina," he said as he walked in the door. "You're gonna love it."

John and Eric were headed for the living room. "No," Christina said. "Not there, the media room. Let's watch it now. I can't wait another minute!"

Both the guys smiled and followed her to the media room. John and Christina sat back in eager anticipation to watch the movie as Eric put in the DVD, turned on the wide-screen TV, and dimmed the lights. "Wait!" Christina called out. Stop the movie!"

"What?" John and Eric both said in disbelief.

"I want to make notes." She left the room and returned with a pen and a notepad. "Okay, roll it," she commanded playfully. During the film, she seemed to be scribbling constantly on her notepad in the dim, flickering light from the movie.

"How can you enjoy the film if you're continually writing?" John asked. Why don't you just sit back and watch it?"

"I'm making notes of things that aren't right," she said in an irritated tone, then went back to writing.

When the movie was over and the credits had finished rolling, Eric switched on the light. John got up and lifted Christina's notepad from her lap. He rifled through the pages of scribbled notes. He stopped at one page and shook his head. "Move the chair a foot to the left?" He tore off the pages of notes from the pad, ripped them in half, crumpled them up into a ball and threw them at the wastebasket near the projector.

"What are you doing!" she screamed as she rose up out of her chair. "Those are my notes! The things I want changed!"

"The movie is perfect," John said quietly. "It's a wrap, Eric. Great job!" He shook Eric's hand. "Can we keep this copy?"

"Sure. It's yours. You paid for it."

John said, "Let's find something to eat." They left Christina there trying to flatten out her wrinkled notes and headed for the kitchen. Christina looked at the notes and sighed. She tossed them in the wastebasket and followed the men into the kitchen.

"I guess that's it, then, Eric. John thinks it's perfect. I was probably a little overzealous in my criticisms."

"It's okay, Christina. I get that all the time in my job. The movie is probably not as perfect as John said, but it's as close as we can get."

They had sandwiches and discussed the promotional angle, then Eric said he'd better turn in. "You don't mind if I stay in the pool house tonight, do you? I gotta catch a 6:30 flight back in the morning."

"Of course not, Eric," Christina said. "You're welcome any time."

"Thanks, Christina. I got a bill here. It includes the projected promotional costs we're going to incur."

"I'll get my checkbook."

John and Christina looked over the bill and then Christina got her checkbook and made out a check for the full amount. She handed it to Eric. "Thank you so much for working on our movie." She gave him a hug. "You're helping to save the world."

Eric stifled a laugh. "I don't know about that, but I think I helped produce a good, entertaining film. Probably not an award winner, but good anyhow."

"I'll walk you out to the pool house," John said. "Do you want to come along, Christina?"

"No, I'll stay here and clean up the kitchen. Will we see you at the premiere, Eric?"

"I'll be there."

John walked Eric over to the pool house, then headed back to the house. He stopped to enjoy the light of the full moon playing on the landscape. He ambled through the orchard over to the ridge to get a grander view. Suddenly a large object shining silver in the moonlight rose up off the ground and into the air above him, revealing red and blue pulsating lights underneath. It accelerated rapidly as it ascended into the sky and disappeared from view.

He hurried to the house, not knowing if Christina had seen the object. If she hadn't, he wasn't going to tell her. She'd be extremely upset to know the spacecraft had been back.

As soon as he touched the door handle, she opened the door. She was bubbling over with excitement. "It's gone! It's gone forever! They won't be back. I can feel it—the oppression and fear I've felt for so long has lifted! Free at last!"

"What? Did you see them go?"

"No. I felt it."

"When?"

"Just now. Just before you got to the door."

John sat down at the kitchen table. He toyed with a tiny crumb left from dinner.

"John! Aren't you happy, excited? What's bothering you?"

"Just thinking. I'll tell you. The spacecraft was back. I saw it take off before I came in the house. And you didn't see it?"

"I told you no, I didn't see it. I was busy with the dishes."

"It makes me wonder. Maybe you were right after all about an alien presence on earth. It's an unsettling thought."

"So you're finally going to believe me. I wonder what made them decide to leave, after all their plans for a takeover."

"I don't know," John said. "Maybe they saw the movie. You know, if there was one ship, others might come here. Let me know if you have any weird dreams in the future." He got up and embraced her. "I love you," he whispered in her ear.

"You didn't love me when you thought I was crazy?"

"Yes, I did. I said so."

"I never heard it."

"You must be crazy if you don't remember that. Women are supposed to remember every little word a man utters, for better or worse."

"Now that you've said it, I'll say it, too. I love you, John. You've been so patient with me, even though you didn't believe me about the aliens."

"That makes me very happy." He kissed her solidly on her lips.

"There's something else I want to tell you. I've changed my mind about the cats. I don't want cats now."

"I'm glad to hear it."

"Instead of cats, I want a baby."

—∿∿—

The spaceship was well away from earth in a few minutes. A lot of alien cursing was going on in that ship. "#@**^%$#$^^%$#@ I've wanted to kill that girl for so long, but I was blocked at every turn. We finally intercept their electronic transmission and find out what they've been up to, and what is it but a movie outlining my whole plan for taking over! I've studied their culture for years, finally found a way to take over earth without a fight—through a god returning to earth, pretending to turn it into a paradise, and what happens?" The humanoid-looking alien with an oversized cranium slams the console with his fist. "Ouch! It's all in that film we just saw," he said to his companion.

"Yeah," the other alien said. "Too bad. That's the third planet we tried to take over but failed. What is it?"

"It's Hezeus. That damned do-gooder! He's always one step ahead of us, spying on us, planting dreams and ideas in his people's heads to spoil our plans, blocking our ability to track them down and kill them!"

"Well, I'm nearly bankrupt now. I can't afford to finance any more of your stupid expeditions. We're going to have to give up the sex toy business and go back to selling space junk."

They looked at the sun diminishing to a tiny dot on their view screen. "Goodbye, Earth people, you #@** stupid tiny-brained animals!" The credits of the movie finished rolling and their screen faded to black.

—∿∿—

About the Author

Christina Vaughan, aka C. C. Vaughan, was born in Pawhuska, Oklahoma. Her first six years were spent on her parents' cattle ranch. Then they moved to Bartlesville, Oklahoma, where she lived until after college at Oklahoma State University. Then she moved to her mother's native city of San Francisco, and later the North Bay. A pianist, Christina studied music in college, as well as creative writing, but preferred editing and writing. She's an editor, book designer and publishing coordinator for self-published authors. She has written 14 You-Draw-It Books, 4 children's novels, and the adult novel *Sky Moon*.

Christina lives in Sonoma County with her pianist/composer husband Robert Ellis. She has a son, Colin Lipper, a Chemistry PhD candidate at UC San Diego, a daughter-in-law, Hope who is a fine arts design graduate, and a "granddog" Bruce, a French Bulldog.